MARK WATSON

THE PLACE THAT DIDN'T EXIST

PICADOR

First published 2016 by Picador

First published in paperback 2016 by Picador

This edition published 2017 by Picador
an imprint of Pan Macmillan
The Smithson, 6 Briset Street, London EC1M 5NR
EU representative: Macmillan Publishers Ireland Limited,
1st Floor, The Liffey Trust Centre, 117-126 Sheriff Street, Upper Dublin 1 D01 YC43
Associated companies throughout the world
www.panmacmillan.com

ISBN 978-1-4472-4337-3

3 5 7 9 8 6 4 2

A CIP catalogue record for this book is available from the British Library.

Typeset by Ellipsis, Glasgow
Printed and bound by CPI Group (UK) Ltd, Croydon, CR0 4YY

Visit **www.picador.com** to read more about all our books
and to buy them. You will also find features, author interviews and
news of any author events, and you can sign up for e-newsletters
so that you're always first to hear about our new releases.

PROLOGUE

'You know the riddle of the dollar?' the Fixer asked, looking around the table.

He laced his long fingers into a pyramid. 'So. Three guests check in to a hotel, like we just checked in here. The guy behind the desk says it's $30, so they each pay ten. Later the clerk realizes he overcharged them: it should have been $25. So he gives the bellboy five bucks to return to the guests. Obviously he can't divide it equally. He keeps $2 for himself. Gives one dollar back to everyone. So they have all paid nine dollars now, yes?'

Everyone agreed that this was true.

'And the bellboy has two. So they've paid nine times three, twenty-seven. He has two. But we started with thirty. So where is the missing dollar?'

The group's attempts to wrestle with the problem began energetically. Someone remembered having heard the riddle before, but her patchy recollection of the solution meant that she ended up confusing everyone even further. Someone grumbled that he hated number puzzles, and it was bad enough that there were Sudokus wherever you looked. The director began to sketch out a solution on a napkin. One person told a story about his struggles with Maths at school; he'd panicked so much during an exam that all he could write was the number 33, over and over again. This led to a general exchange of schooldays mishaps, and before long focus had slipped from the dollar question altogether.

This was understandable; it had been a long day of travelling, and Dubai, they could tell already, was a place of distractions. The air had a delicious hot-country smell which had surrounded them as soon as they'd got out of the airport a couple of hours ago: a juicy, spiced aroma which evoked holidays or adventures, even though they were there to work. A baby grand piano had been wheeled out onto the terrace in front of them, and an amplifier set up; a fifty-something woman in a red dress and a weaselly keyboard player had appeared. The woman said that it was time to grab a drink or three – she paused for the witticism to sink in – and get ready to enjoy some classics.

Besides, they were all hungry, keen to eat before the welcome speech began, and the buffet was bewilderingly extensive. It spread over an archipelago of outdoor tables, and the aromas of different cuisines met and mingled in mouthwatering fashion. It was about twenty minutes before every member of the team had navigated this kingdom of food and loaded up a tray, and by that time the dollar riddle lay on the roadside of the conversation, with no chance of making a comeback.

If the dollar riddle ever came to mind after that, it was as a comforting footnote, something to dwell on for a little while as an escape from the confusion we found ourselves in. Those of us who were left, that is.

PART ONE

1: WE ARE GOING TO CHANGE LIVES

They had left Heathrow on a morning so gloomy it could have passed for dusk, and now ten hours later it was the opposite: a blue-purple night which felt like day. On the drive through Dubai, lights were everywhere, tracing the improbable outlines of the buildings Tim had seen on the internet, but was nonetheless startled by. One tower resembled a tulip, its head a wreath of steel petals; others had arrowed tops like open blades about to slash at the sky, or seemed to change shape altogether halfway up. The skyline was green, purple; colours no one expected. And now, here in the Village resort, there were festoon lights coiled around trees, as if the place existed in a permanent state of festivity. Lanterns marked out the paths.

As he looked over the heads of those opposite, over the terrace, Tim could see in the distance the Burj Al Arab, Dubai's most famous landmark, spaceship-like in appearance and picked out by pin-sharp lines of bulbs which alternated red and blue. He'd kept an image of the building on his computer desktop for weeks, as he looked forward to the trip; it was hard to make his brain understand that this was the real thing. Nothing, in fact, felt completely real. Tim found it astonishing to think that tomorrow he would wake up in a lilypad of a bed, in a sun-warmed chalet nestling among pools and swim-up bars, while his colleagues at home would be struggling onto buses and walking head down through spitting autumn rain. He looked around the table at his new teammates and could hardly stop a grin from stealing onto his face.

Christian Roper cleared his throat to begin his welcome address. Somehow, though it was almost inaudible, it had the same effect as somebody tapping on a glass, and the table went quiet. 'So,' he said, 'just a little bit in the way of form- alities. Firstly, welcome. Welcome one and all. Jo and I – and everyone at WorldWise – are excited you're here. We have the chance to launch a great campaign here. In fact, not even a great one: a superb one. A superb one.'

Roper had a politician's staccato delivery, and the same way of making forced eye contact, but the effect – Tim thought – was much warmer than politicians generally achieved. He still had the gift for connecting with listeners that had made him a TV personality in the nineties, before the switch into activism and philanthropy that prompted Tim's parents to complain that he had 'gone a bit serious these days' whenever he appeared on the news. He was not as tall as Tim had imagined, but he was the sort of person to grow in stature with an audience.

'As you all know, tomorrow we have a big star arriving: the amazing Jason Streng. We have a very strong concept.' Roper gestured at Tim, whose concept it was, and Tim allowed himself a quiet shiver of satisfaction. 'And the stakes could not be higher. The world has never needed this charity more. There are children dying; people starving. We are going to change lives, ladies and gentlemen.'

He paused for exactly the right length of time, so that the statement sounded weighty but not too bombastic. 'So I was thinking that we could all introduce ourselves. Your name, your role on the project, and maybe just one interesting fact about yourself. Shall we go round? I'll start: I'm Christian Roper, founder and CEO of WorldWise.'

'*Co*-founder,' Jo murmured, but Christian went on. 'And my fact: I'm planning to run a marathon next year but a part of me fears I'm too old. Just too old. Don't all rush to correct me at once!' He laughed, and the people around the table made efforts of varying merit to laugh with him.

'Jo. Communications director for WorldWise,' said Christian's wife, whom Tim also recognized from the website. Like Christian, she was as impressive in person as in the online images of the Ropers presiding over charitable ventures in the developing world: she had very dark eyes, which Tim felt were squarely on his face, and the sort of cheekbones associated with models. 'Long-suffering wife. And my fact is that I've met two American presidents. That's if Obama wins. Which he will.'

Tim was beginning to feel alarmed by the request for 'one interesting fact'. He had been in this position once before, when he'd rashly signed up for Drama Society at university. One girl had used the opportunity to discuss her history of anxiety and self-harm, another had spent her minute expressing support for the first girl, and by the time it got round to Tim, his claim to have captained the school's chess team rang rather hollow.

What were you meant to say in these situations, if your life had been without major incident so far? Tim began to envy people who'd been born with an extra toe or revived from a coma. Silently he auditioned possible revelations. I have a brother who worked in the City and – well, we don't see him much any more. My father curates a model village. I used to do orienteering; represented the county at under-16 level. None of it seemed substantial enough. At least, to his relief, they were going the opposite way around the circle, so he could listen to the other disclosures first.

The head cameraman was next to speak. He was a burly,

amiable-looking man with hair fashioned into a rockabilly quiff. He'd shown up at the airport already in khaki shorts, despite the cold, and wore a T-shirt referencing a sci-fi show Tim had half heard of.

'Miles Aldridge: director of photography. My fact is, I can recite *The Empire Strikes Back* word for word. And I do mean word for word.'

'Ruth Lingard: AP. Which of course stands for, erm, stands for assistant producer.' This was a woman of about forty who had sat next to Tim in the airport car. He had noted, there, her habit of interrupting herself in the middle of sentences, and her mass of red hair. 'I once caught a burglar busting into my nana's place and got on top of him and pinned him down till the cops came.'

'My real name is Ali,' declared the Fixer. 'My job is less clearly defined than any of yours; to be brief, I do whatever is necessary for the project. I have ridden a zebra. Which is said to be impossible. I have also eaten zebra. Not the same one.' The Fixer grinned and adjusted his Panama hat. Since collecting them from the airport he had done a lot of grinning, as if this whole ad campaign were a practical joke whose payoff he expected to see any time soon.

'Raf Kavanagh: producer. I slept with a very famous actress before she got famous. I won't name names. Except to say her name's Kate and the surname rhymes with Dinslet.'

There was laughter at this. Raf had spent the flight in first class, rather than business like the rest of them, having argued his way up at check-in by wielding a nexus of frequent flyer points. He had gel-sculpted hair and a shirt of obvious expensiveness. On the approach to the hotel, along the car-choked Sheikh Zayed Road, his mobile had gone off, the ringtone a song which had only been released that week. 'I'm in Dubai,' he'd shouted, while the other passengers made a faux-pretence of not noticing, or minding. 'I know: fucking *Dubai*!'

Tim felt increasingly uncomfortable as the baton passed to the small man on his right, Bradley. He had sat next to Tim on the flight, drinking can after can of Coke Zero and reading a book on silent movies, never once removing the baseball cap which covered his bald head. Tim did not like to break a silence, and the same was clearly true of Bradley, so for the entire seven hours the two men did not exchange a word: an arrangement they'd both been happy with.

'Bradley Ford Richards: director. I've worked in commercial production for more than fifteen years. In that time I've worked for Budweiser, CNN, Sony. I—'

'We just need a fact, not a CV,' said Raf Kavanagh, breaking in.

'Excuse me?' The American blinked, surprised.

'A résumé,' Ruth explained. 'He means we don't need a résumé.'

'Oh.' Bradley ran his tongue slowly over his lips. 'OK.'

He did not offer another fact, and there was a brief, edgy silence, which suited Tim well: it meant that everyone was relieved when he took his turn. 'I'm Tim Callaghan,' he said, very aware of his own voice; by misfortune the musical backdrop had fallen away, as the middle-aged singer had announced a break after a laboured 'Girl From Ipanema'.

'I work for Vortex – for the ad agency. Anyway. My fact is that I sleepwalk, and also get quite heavy nosebleeds. Not connected.'

This made little obvious impact, even with the almost-quirky final line, and he wondered whether he should have gone for the orienteering. Still, it was done, and Tim reached for the bottle of wine in front of him. He sloshed out a glassful as the momentary pressure of the situation fluttered away from his shoulders. For a second, his foot brushed against Jo's under the table. He looked up into the sky, which was extravagantly dotted with stars, and heard or imagined the gentle swish of the sea on the private beach just below their terrace. I am incredibly lucky, he thought for the second time in half an hour.

Or perhaps it wasn't luck. Stan, Tim's boss, had always said that their job was about telling stories, and that if you were good enough at it, they became reality. This seemed pompous or just plain silly to the many people who looked down on the advertising industry: Tim's brother Rod had described it as 'money for nothing' even though he himself, as a City trader, had once earned £50,000 with three clicks of the mouse button. Still, however merited it might look to an outsider, Tim had a right to the pride, or at least the sense of accomplishment, which he felt building slowly inside him. His vision had helped to assemble the experienced team that sat around this table. He'd told a story in which he was flown to Dubai to oversee a glamorous project, and now here he was in the middle of it. It was as much as he could do to avoid beaming again, like a simpleton, at his new workmates.

When Tim remembered these moments, months and years later, it would be as one might look back on a family gathering just before a life-changing drama: with wonderment at how little he and everyone knew at the time, and perhaps a yearning for that ignorance.

2: CREDIT

It had all begun the previous year, in 2007, when Tim's boss Stan told him that Visit Dubai were coming in for a meeting. They had a startling budget and a simple brief: appropriately, it was to make people visit Dubai. Really, every brief ought to be that simple, but clients were sometimes squeamish about the idea that they were hiring an ad agency to make them money. They talked instead of 'building the brand', of 'narratives' and 'deliverables'. By filling meetings with this sort of jargon they successfully shielded everyone from the embarrassment of saying what the meeting was actually about.

The Dubai delegation had no such inhibitions. They sent graphs to show how many people currently holidayed in Dubai (already a surprising number) and what they would like the figure to be in five years (considerably higher). Their key message – what Stan called the 'take-home' – was that Dubai was easy to get to, suitable for families, and above all hot: hotter than the Canaries or even Barbados, hot with a clinical reliability, insuring tourists against what they most feared: disappointment. There was a note that 'approaches with humour' would be preferred. Vortex, Tim's agency, was given a week to think about this and then invited to pitch ideas over lunch at the Ivy Club.

Although his title was still Junior Creative, Tim was getting more and more of these briefs to work on, having recently masterminded a campaign for Yorkshire Tourism. The ad was thirty seconds long: it featured a bored-out-of-their-minds couple sitting wordlessly in a modern, very white lounge. One received a text, answered it; the other did the same. The silence continued. The camera cut to a magnificent Dales vista and the caption GO OUTSIDE INSTEAD. The client loved it, Tim was nominated at the Tourism and Travel Viral Campaign Awards, and nobody ever found out that the shot they'd used was actually of the Peak District.

With this credit behind him, Tim was given the Dubai brief to work on. He'd heard about the place, of course. Household names, looked up after 'where are they now?' debates, often proved to have retired there; it was favoured as a holiday destination by super-rich, semi-mythical figures like the Beckhams; pictures of its skyline, the seven-star Burj Al Arab, were used in broadsheet supplements to support stories about the shifting world economy. Still, it was only in the course of his research for this job that Tim learned just how rich the city was – and not just rich but self-consciously and competitively so. Alongside the predictable sun-and-beach shots brought up by Google Images, the skyscraper-dwarfing towers, the living spaces full of crystalline polygons and peopled by happy humans of differing ethnicities, there was a lot of what he recognized as PR-speak. 'Dubai's rise and rise is one of the great modern success stories,' one website remarked. 'In Dubai, desire and reality are the same thing,' claimed another. There was a lot of talk of 'iconic' buildings, and at least four developments were described as 'once-in-a-generation'. Fortunately for Tim, this building of a mythology was not his business for now. He just had to get across that it was sunny.

He searched 'sunshine holidays' on the internet and happened upon a travel anecdotes site where someone described squirting suntan lotion onto their food on a self-catering trip, believing it was salad cream. The lady confessed that she'd tried eating a bit of it because she was 'too hot to bother cooking anything else'. This gave him the idea for a Dubai strapline: IT'S TOO HOT TO WORRY! The ads Tim proposed would show holidaymakers so pleasurably addled by the climate that they grabbed an ice-cream by the wrong end, wore shorts back to front, tried to drive their car in the sea like a pedalo. After submitting this idea, Vortex were put on the shortlist, and summoned to a meeting with a bright-eyed Arab man in a spotless Armani suit.

'I like the idea very much,' said the client, as soon as the discussion began. Tim's heart sank.

'There is just one reservation,' the man went on, as Tim had known he would. 'Too hot to worry. I wonder if people are seeing that and thinking: it will be too hot.'

Tim knew the trick in these situations was to agree with the client's idiotic point of view while continuing to argue with it. 'I see what you mean,' he said, 'but we're not saying it's "too hot" per se. We're just . . . just using a bit of humour.'

He was sent away to rework the idea and came up with WHEN IT'S THIS HOT, YOU CAN LOSE TRACK! The feedback was that 'losing track' might be a worrying idea, suggesting misplaced passports and forgotten flight details. He changed tack and went for THESE THINGS HAPPEN IN THE SUN. The client emailed that he was 'still concerned about this emphasis on sun,' even though the original brief had mentioned little else. Tim suggested a couple of blander, non-meteorological lines. Vortex heard nothing for a while, then an email arrived regretting that Visit Dubai had 'chosen another partner for this journey'. He eventually saw the winning design splashed across the wall of an underground station; the slogan they'd picked was FLY TO DUBAI.

'Still,' said Tim's boss, Stan, who tended to be optimistic

about everything other than the impact of his young children on his marriage, 'we've put credit in the bank with those guys.'

There was always a lot of talk in their office about 'credit' – a word that could get you anything, from mobile call-time to a house, and more nebulous commodities like self-esteem. Sometimes it felt to Tim as if words like 'credit' and 'market' were nothing more than that, words: concrete nouns that had been beaten up into abstracts. But sometimes they became solid again. In April 2008, an email arrived saying that Tim's name had been favourably mentioned – by whom it did not specify – and the Dubai-based charity WorldWise was inviting him to pitch for a TV ad soliciting online donations. 'The inequalities of our planet are unbelievable,' said the email. 'Can it really be that by 2016, 1 per cent of the world's population will own 99 per cent of its wealth? With a budget for a major star, and a wide range of distribution options, we are looking for an idea that uses humour to bring this extremely serious statistic to light.'

'Good luck making *that* funny,' remarked Tim's flatmate Pete, absently reading the printout that Tim had left on their kitchen table. Pete had come back drunk from the pub, as he did almost every night; he had entered the teaching profession hoping to make a positive difference to the world, but instead the job had made a negative difference to him.

'I'd like to get this,' said Tim, staring for the tenth time at the promotional image at the foot of the email: Christian Roper with a shovel slung over his shoulder, a lean and brown Jo next to him, the pair seemingly inspecting a newly built well. At the bottom of the image were remarkable statistics about the total money raised by WorldWise, the number of people they'd supplied with housing or essential medicines, and so on. 'It looks like it'll be huge. Also,' he added, 'I mean, the poverty stuff. Ninety-nine per cent of the . . . it's pretty astonishing, that.'

'Mmm,' Pete agreed. 'I spilled some mayo on it, by the way.'

Inspiration often struck Tim by stealth when he was bathing or getting his clothes ready for the following morning, but it was noticeably absent over the next couple of days. The more Tim tried to wrestle ideas into being, the more they squirmed away; but when he used reverse psychology and tried not to have an idea, his brain called his bluff by not having one.

On his way to the Shoreditch office two days after the initial email, Tim walked past a man huddled in a doorway, a cardboard sign in front of him: I AM VERY HUNGRY! Commuters in their various forms went by: financiers in tailored suits, prematurely bearded young men on their way to serve shifts as baristas. There was no animosity in the way they glanced at the man, or in the way they disregarded his pleas for change; rather, it was as if he wasn't there at all. Tim, as he handed over a pound, wondered whether the man did this every morning and it was only now, because of this charity campaign playing on his mind, that Tim had noticed him. He took the lift up to the open-plan office on the sixth floor, where an East End artist had arranged – with deliberate un-evenness – the words VORTEX (NOUN): A PLACE WHERE NORMAL LAWS DO NOT APPLY in red fibreglass under the Vortex logo, and where espresso machines and football tables bore witness to the fact that Stan had been on a course about 'Making Your Workplace Unique'. As Tim sat down at his Mac, Stan asked how the WorldWise pitch was going.

'I'm nearly there,' said Tim, waiting for Stan to move away before he opened the Word file in which he'd so far only writ-ten four words.

That night he tried to explain to Pete why seeing the home-less man had struck him as significant. 'It's the sort of thing you see and just forget, or don't even register, but there's something awful about it. A guy who once had parents, and . . . and plans for the future, all that. And now his only plan is to sit there with a sign saying that he's hungry. While people just ignore him. I mean, I gave him a quid, but I'm not going to do that every day.'

'He'd only spend it on booze,' Pete consoled him.

'So would you.'

Pete accepted this with two raised palms. 'More to the point, when did you – as an advertiser – start getting a . . . what's it called . . .?'

'A social conscience?'

'Yes.'

'I don't know.' Tim reached for the bottle of wine, which was worryingly light after its evening with Pete. 'Maybe it's an early mid-life crisis.'

That night he struggled to sleep. The image of the man in the doorway troubled him; in some way he stood for the vast ranks of unknown human suffering that WorldWise mentioned in their brief, and reminded Tim how little he engaged with that suffering. Of course, you could not help everyone, and that was why the majority of people walked heedlessly past the I AM VERY HUNGRY! man. Nobody's windscreen left space for more than a sliver of scenery not related to their own existence; a laptop malfunction in one's own life seemed as weighty as a bereavement in someone else's. In many ways this was a matter of self-defence against the overwhelming range and intractability of problems. There was horror everywhere in the wider world, most of it beyond the ordinary person's capacity to affect. There were countless political prisoners, refugees, people starving; and if it was impossible to change everything, which it was, it soon became the rational decision to change nothing.

That doesn't mean you don't have a 'social conscience', Tim told himself. It just makes you normal. An ordinary person can't possibly process the fact that the world is so full of misery. It's – what had they said in the WorldWise brief? – unbelievable.

He groped for his glasses on the bedside table, snapped on the light and reached for the printout. *The inequalities of our planet are unbelievable.* 'There you go!' he said out loud, hearing Pete's groan from the other side of the wall: Pete was used to these occasional declamations when ideas struck.

By the time he exited the station the next morning, in slanting rain, Tim had the concept. *Believe the unbelievable.* The star of the ad would walk down the street naked, or take flight and swoop over it. Bystanders would be seen gawping, and then adjusting to the situation: buying the star a pint as he landed, offering a coat to preserve his modesty. When we see the unbelievable with our own eyes – the ad would suggest – we are forced to accept it. Yet every day we see the inequalities of the world we live in. Why can't we acknowledge those?

Tim wrote three pages on this idea and gave them to Stan to send in. Where the tourism project had been point-lessly drawn out, this was unusually straightforward. Within a couple of days, Tim was given a Skype appointment with Christian Roper himself.

When he appeared in his box on the screen, Roper was wearing a blue designer shirt. Sunlight streamed over his face, at times obscuring his features altogether. He sat in a glossy white kitchen with a row of pots and pans above his head: a style decision perhaps inspired by the Wiltshire farmhouse where Roper had grown up, but more likely inspired by other wealthy people with displays of rustic-looking kitchenware in their own homes.

Christian Roper said that he loved the idea of the ad; he just needed to get the go-ahead from his funders.

'But the main funder,' said Roper with a wolfish smile, 'is myself.'

'Then I hope the conversation with yourself goes well,' said Tim. Christian Roper threw his head back and laughed; Tim felt the rare exhilaration of a landed joke.

He was used to dampening his expectations. If there was a rule by which you could survive in this job, it was that you should disregard everything anyone said, and the more encouraging or enthusiastic they were, the less you should trust them. All the same, Tim had a success-ticker which clicked into gear at times like this. It tick-tacked through the next few days, distracting him in the office, causing his ruffled mind to take him sleepwalking one night; he woke in the process of putting bread into the toaster. He said nothing further about it to Pete (who had problems of his own, to do with a pupil who'd brought a samurai sword into school) or to his mum (because she worried about the sustainability of his career, and sometimes sent leaflets for law conversion courses in the post). This was advertising. Most things, as Stan liked to say, never happened.

Almost a week after the Skype interview, Tim's phone lit up during Sunday lunch with Pete and some other friends in a three-centuries-old pub in Clapham. The pub had been modernized in recent times with a brasserie menu and a big projector screen for sports events, but it was now under-going a refurbishment to make it seem old again. The call was from Stan, who would never normally ring on a Sunday; Tim's heart accelerated. He took the phone out to the toilets, where the re-exposed brickwork was covered in sepia pictures of industrialists who'd once lived in the area.

'We got Dubai,' said Stan.

Tim punched the air and gave a brief yell, like a tennis player. A woman came out of the toilets and he tried to make it look as if the yell had been a sneeze.

'Now, thing is,' Stan added, 'normally I'd go over. But you know how much I'm in the doghouse if I'm not back for bedtime. Louise nearly shot me for going to Chingford the other day; I don't think I'm going to get away with the Middle East.'

Tim experienced a clutch of anxious excitement as he realized what was coming next. 'Do you fancy it, mate?'

Tim took a moment, after the call, to digest what he had just learned: not only that he'd earned Vortex a gigantic account, but that he himself was being offered a week-long trip to a destination he'd never imagined visiting before, and which all his research had suggested was sensational. It was one of his secret embarrassments that he hadn't travelled anywhere near as much as most people he spoke to at parties, who traded stories of Cancún and Cambodia. His own globetrotting experience was limited to a summer in Australia with his older brother, a parade of cheap hotels and hung-over coach trips which seemed cruelly distant now he hardly ever heard from Rod; and, more recently, a romantic sojourn in New York which had ended the romance. His girlfriend Naomi had undergone a series of epiphanies in the Big Apple, the most crucial one being that she was going to stay there, specifically with a barman called Moses whom they'd met on the second night. That had been two years ago, and since then Tim had not ventured far, either in love or in geographical terms. But now, out of nowhere, there was this.

The others were emphatic – or jealous – in their congratulations when he returned to the table. 'You absolute bastard,' said Pete's friend Duncan. 'Du-fucking-bai!'

'It should be nice,' Tim conceded.

'Should be?' Duncan shook his head. 'Dubai is the business. Hot every day, place is clean as fuck, all the expats are getting plastered every night, they have an underwater restaurant, seven-star hotel, you name it, mate. You can literally do anything there.'

And as Tim reviewed his first evening here, after they had retired from the terrace, this was already starting to seem true. Placing tomorrow's clothes ready in a pile – a ritual that dated from his early schooldays, when he'd dreaded the moment of leaving the duvet's warmth – Tim looked around his accommodation. Above the bed, which would have felt roomy for two people, hung a neon-drenched skyline print of the city, and monochrome pictures of a bygone Dubai: a wizened falconer, a group of men hauling a dhow into the water. A giant TV hovered like a moon orbiting a planet: THE VILLAGE WELCOMES MR CALLAGHAN! enthused the screen, with a smaller caption instructing him to call 234 for all his needs. There was a bathroom twice the size of the one he had at home, a separate lounge with a dining table and minibar, and a terrace with a deckchair outside.

It was probably time for Tim to text Pete and admit that this was the biggest stroke of good fortune he could have had. But the bed already felt as if it had adapted to his body-shape and would never let him go.

3: SERVICE

Someone was knocking. They knocked three times, and then a key was in the door. Tim, unused to such deep sleep, woke with no idea of what time it was – or, for a moment, where he was. He rolled out of bed and tried to open the blinds, but they would not budge; the bedside light wouldn't even come on. He threw on a T-shirt. A small man was standing in the doorway to the bedroom, clearing his throat in practised apology.

'Sir, am I disturbing?'

'Not at all,' said Tim drowsily, though it was hard to say what 'disturbing' might mean if not this. 'I was just . . .'

'I am Ashraf, sir.' The man wore a green T-shirt with the Village's logo, and sported an eccentric curling moustache, the sort of thing people at Tim's work occasionally cultivated as a sort of kitsch half-joke. 'And how is your stay so far, Mr Callag . . . er, Callag . . .'

'Callaghan,' said Tim. 'The G is a red herring.'

'I'm sorry, sir – if you would repeat . . .?'

'The G . . . I just mean it's a silent G.'

He saw Ashraf decide not to grapple any further with this issue; instead, he launched into a speech. 'Sir, because of the late hours of your arrival, it has not been possible yesterday to conduct your Village initiation. Is this a suitable time instead?'

'It's fine,' said Tim, glancing down at his underwear, 'although I'm not actually—'

'Thank you very much, sir.' Ashraf was already standing next to the bed, toying with an LCD panel flat against the wall. 'You have seen that this panel is for the operation of the blind and lights, and also illuminates the DO NOT DISTURB sign outside if you are wishing to do activities in private.' Tim, crouching by his suitcase for a pair of shorts, had barely registered any of this when Ashraf was on to his next demonstration, featuring another panel – this time built into the wall of the lounge. 'Here is how we control mood lighting and music, if music is necessary.' A couple of button-presses effected a swoop of ceiling spotlights and three seconds of a Dido song, both of which were gone again before Tim had seen how they were created. Ashraf went on to show how air-conditioning was controlled – he left it on, at what seemed an uncomfortably high level to Tim – and proceeded to the bathroom, still speaking in manicured but fractionally inaccurate English, like an instruction manual.

'Here is where we are leaving towels, if towels are wishing to be changed, but we are considering the environment.'

The shower was the finale of the tour: it featured ten settings, including Tropical Storm and London Rain. Tim watched politely as Ashraf showed off the former, pressing a button to unleash a series of synthesized rumbles and a dramatic increase in water-pressure.

Back in the lounge, Ashraf laid a printed sheet on the coffee table.

'This is a satisfaction questionnaire, sir, in which you can explain everything that was good and not so good about this initiation.'

There was something plaintive about the request, and Tim promised that he would.

'And wishing you a very great stay at the Village and please call 234 if there are any needs.'

Feeling a little punch-drunk from the extent of his welcome, Tim consulted his itinerary. It was half past ten. They were all meeting at the WorldWise office at five, to go to an event at which the ad's star, Jason Streng – and, unnervingly, Tim's concept – would be unveiled to 'investors and media'. That meant he had most of the day to get his bearings and enjoy being here. He opened the door of his chalet and stepped out into air so warm it was like getting into a bath.

The sky was a digital-looking blue, and the sun had a stolid appearance like a veteran employee midway through a shift. Tim sank down into a deckchair on his terrace to fill out the questionnaire and surveyed the resort. The team working on the ad were in their own enclosure called Ocean Chalets. To the left, a gentle slope led down to the beach and the clump of bars and restaurants where they had been the previous night. The other way led to a tall chrome tower called the Centrepiece, the hub of the Village, where the Fixer had checked them all in, scooping up each individual's paperwork and seemingly dismissing it all with a single word and the wave of a hand.

Tim left Ocean Chalets and stood in front of a plan of the Village. He always liked to get the measure of a new place. His orienteering days had given him an appreciation of cartography, of the body's need to understand its physical surroundings. In New York, his insistence on a long study of the Manhattan *Lonely Planet*, clashing as it did with Naomi's eagerness to charge straight out for spontaneous adventures, had caused an uncharacteristically big row on their first night – the night before she decided to replace him.

The Village had been built a decade ago: by Dubai's standards it was old. People bustled past with towels draped over their arms, and Tim glanced at them with the respect of a newcomer for the old guard. Green-shirted staff circulated, arranging sprinklers on lawns, delivering cocktails to women with cucumber slices over their eyes. Buggies pootled up and down, ferrying elderly or lazy guests. There were palm trees everywhere. All this was much as Tim had expected, although it was rather different from a 'village' like the one he was brought up in, Saddlecombe in Devon, where you couldn't get fish and chips after eight o'clock at night, and an affair conducted by the vicar in 1965 was still widely discussed.

Yet in a way, this place *was* like a village: it aspired to be a community of humans, a place people really lived in, rather than visited. The numerous signs were made of stone and designed to look hand-engraved, as if they were beside a country road in England. Tim stood on the beach, enjoying the unlikeliness of it: sand beneath his shoes and the great expanse of sea, where twenty-four hours ago he'd been in London with the waterproofed charity collectors and pigeons and polite ill-will. A man was tending to the sand with a long, four-pronged rake. Sun-loungers followed the line of the water, but only a few people were here, shielded by parasols, motionless. In a small marina, thirty sparkly white boats sat like abandoned bath-toys. Perched on its own, custom-made island was the Burj Al Arab, chunky but somehow lithe, excitingly alien even by day. He wondered what unimaginable extravagances had won its sixth and seventh stars, and were being unleashed even as he watched from afar.

The Centrepiece seemed a good place to start. Inside, the hot-to-cold transition hit him again. Signage informed him of the different facilities on the tower's various levels: The Body, Mind and Soul Centre, Shop City, Catering Planet. Behind the heads of the reception staff was a photo of Sheikh Mohammed, a hawk-like smile on his face. There was a TV on which images of the Village rotated: a golfer swinging with fine technique at a ball, ice sculptures being shown off to delighted residents. A notice spelled out the Village Service Pledge.

We will welcome with a smile
We will take a joy in service
We will meet all your needs
We will bid a fond farewell

He found his way up to Catering Planet on the sixth floor: it was a sort of upmarket food court, with a menu as thick as a telephone directory advertising a fusion of all imaginable cuisines.

JIMMY'S BURRITOS — straight out of a ranch on the hot, sticky Mexican border.

BOEUF BOURGIGNON — we learned to cook it this way on the banks of the Seine.

FISH AND CHIPS AND MUSHY PEAS — just like in old Blighty! The skies may be grey, but the boys have brought in the catch . . .

Tim's jolted body clock could not tell him whether he should be thinking of this as breakfast or lunch: in the end, he ordered a God Bless the Stars and Stripes Burger. 'That'll be right with you,' said the waitress, and he wondered if she had put on an American accent purely because of his order, and had a repertoire to cover other possibilities. This seemingly absurd idea was lent weight when 'Achy Breaky Heart' abruptly began to play from the speakers. Tim reflected that not far from here, there were people so opposed to the United States that they were prepared to die to make their point; in this environment, though, America – like anything else – was little more than an idea, a collection of shorthands.

Tim's travels had never taken him anywhere quite like this. The Callaghans had generally holidayed on campsites in damp corners of France, Mr Callaghan buying a loaf of bread and some cheese every morning before revealing a punishing schedule of bike-rides. At most there would be one or two cafes near the site, and they'd 'eat out' on the final night. Tim wondered what his parents would make of the Village: a place where, as was already clear, the restaurants and gym facilities were not to serve a destination, but were the destination themselves.

The WorldWise office was on the top floor; Tim stopped in briefly to say hello. He found Ruth and Raf deep in preparation for the arrival of the film star. There was no sign of anyone else from the team, though maybe that was not surprising. The Fixer, Ruth had told him last night, worked to no timetable at all: his contract simply stipulated that he had to be within twenty minutes' reach at all times. 'He's worked on those terms since the Ropers got here,' said Ruth, 'and never once failed.'

'I have Jason to be picked up by Superior Limos at four,' Ruth was saying now into the phone. 'Yes, and his agent.' A pause; she rolled her eyes at Tim. 'Yes, we'll make sure no one speaks directly to Jason.'

'Can you get off the phone and come and look at this?' Raf asked Ruth.

'Could you email it to me?' Ruth mouthed, still listening to the demands of the famous actor's representatives.

'I could,' said Raf, 'or you could do what I'm saying.'

Ruth winced; Tim felt as if he'd witnessed someone being slapped. He backed out of the sliding doors and went in search of the Body, Mind and Soul Centre.

Like many people in London, Tim went to the gym almost passively, as if it were an unavoidable part of being alive. The array of apparatus in the Body, Mind and Soul Centre, however, made him feel as if his gym in Shoreditch belonged in a doll's house. At least a hundred running machines, bikes and cross-trainers were arranged in banks of ten. Above them, TV screens played dozens of channels at once. There was a pop video, a rolling news station – . . . WARN FINANCIAL EXPERTS, said the back-end of a headline – and a horse-race with the caption ENDURANCE CITY. Keening motivational music filled the air: *I wanna get so high*, someone sang. And there was further encouragement on the walls, which were dominated by energizing slogans: THE ONLY BAD WORKOUT IS ONE WHICH DOESN'T HAPPEN.

At the moment, however, a lot of workouts were not happening, since there was almost nobody in sight. The absence of exercisers made the hyperactive music sound a little desperate, like someone trying to get applause from an undersized crowd. As he went to the water-cooler, however, Tim caught sight of Jo. On a crash-mat next to a big soft ball, she was executing press-ups with a grim precision. He thought of last night, when she'd been smoking and drinking more than anyone else. Now, girders of muscle stood out on her arms as she lowered and arched her lean body. He watched her just long enough to feel as if he were doing something inappropriate, and left in search of the 'Mind' and 'Soul' areas.

Here, too, the clientele was sparse: pan-pipe music whistled like wind through a haunted house. A lady in a kimono greeted him from behind an orchid-strewn front desk.

'You would like massage?'

This again was the sort of thing that people were always discussing at work – Stan regularly boasted that he'd 'had the shit beaten out of his back' in Soho – but which Tim himself had never got the hang of. Why not now, he thought. He was far from home. This was a place of possibilities, and already he was unusually relaxed.

'I'd love one,' he said.

He was shown to a room where another woman introduced herself with a single-syllable name he couldn't have transcribed. She gave Tim a cup of hot green tea and casually instructed him to take off all his clothes. 'You will please put these on,' she said, handing him a pair of underpants made of something like crepe paper, 'and lie on table with your head in the hole. Which soundtrack you like?'

He examined the CD case she handed over: the tracks

included 'Secrets of the Forest' and 'The Wondrous Ocean'. It had been made by a company called Weapon, in Basingstoke. He opted for 'Pure Island Bliss'.

Lying as directed with his face staring through a gap at the end of the table, Tim felt at first like a patient awaiting surgery. Without his glasses, the floor was a fuzz below. As soon as her hands spread oil across the small of his back, the helplessness translated itself into pleasurable abandon. He thought how good it was to be touched: not sexual, but warming, human. It was a little while since he'd split with Naomi, and even she had rarely explored his skin with this sort of confidence. He was relieved when the lady began to speak.

'You are working here?'

'Yes,' said Tim, 'making an advert.'

'Advert . . .?'

'A commercial.'

'Oh! Commercial,' said the masseuse, seemingly charmed by the idea, as if he'd said he was looking after wildlife. 'Lot of pressure?'

'Well,' Tim said, 'any job has its pressures, I guess, but no, my role is really just to supervise the—'

'No, pressure like this,' she clarified, applying her fingers a little harder to his shoulder-blades. Tim felt himself colour.

'Oh, I see. Er – this is perfect, thanks.'

'Can try a little more pressure for the extreme relaxing,' she suggested. Tim agreed. The masseuse sprang with feline suddenness onto the table, and drove the point of her elbow into the middle of his back so forcefully that he gasped.

'No, I think . . . back to the one before.'

For forty minutes he lay in a state of sleep-like repose, punctuated by the occasional sensation of pure pleasure. He thought yet again how remarkable it was that he could be doing this while normal people were at work. But the thought was as out of focus as all the others; off it went like flotsam.

Afterwards, it felt as though no one would ever make a loud noise again. Tim sat for five minutes in a curtained enclave, sipping more green tea, clad in a dressing-gown. When at last he stood up to leave, and drew back the curtain, he started in shock: Jo was sitting in a wicker armchair with an American newspaper – some headline, again, about the markets – in a gown just like his. He glanced involuntarily at her bare ankles. Jo laughed.

'You should have told me! We could have gone together!'

The joke sounded flirtatious. Tim had to remind himself that she was the client, a massively important client.

'I didn't plan on a massage,' he said, somewhat sheep-ishly.

'You don't need to plan!' Her face relaxed when she smiled, becoming almost girlish; but it tightened again quickly, as if she didn't like to be caught like that. 'You're on holiday.'

'Not really. It's meant to be work.'

'*I'm* meant to be working.' Jo sipped her glass of water with a wry expression. 'But I'll be at it till god-knows-what-o-clock tonight, networking with all the ghastly people at the launch. I mean, sorry, valued partners. So, right now is playtime.'

'How often do you come here?'

'Is that a pick-up line? "Do you come here often?"' She was enjoying his discomfort, he felt, and it was possible he was enjoying that in turn. 'Work out every day; spa every day as a reward.'

'It's quite a place, this,' said Tim.

'You don't know the half of it,' said Jo. 'And you'll get a bit of a look at Dubai itself tonight.'

He said he would see her there, and picked his way past saunas, where electrically fired furnaces strained to maintain a temperature only a few degrees higher than the temperature outside. At the desk, he tried to pay for the massage, but the kimono lady shook her head with a soft smile. 'Is already paid for.'

'I don't think—'

'By the man, the Fixer.'

As he waited for the lift, Tim tried to work out how the Fixer could possibly have seen him entering the massage place, and why he would have made arrangements to pay for something that was clearly not part of the ad's budget. There was no way of answering these questions, and such was Tim's state of relaxation that he didn't consider them for more than a moment.

The chalet had been so meticulously serviced that it was as if Tim had never set foot there. The air-conditioning purred happily to itself; on the bed, the sheets had been lined up with geometric precision. A pineapple, sliced, sat in a bowl: it was Fruit of the Day, according to a note which went on to describe where pineapples were grown and how they could be used in cooking. Tim left the chalet door open, unwilling to part entirely with the luxury of everything outside. He could hear music floating out of the beachside bars. The afternoon felt like a huge cushion on which he could lie for as long as he wanted.

4: THE FUTURE IS TODAY

Ruth and Bradley were already waiting outside the Centre-piece, although Tim had got there a few minutes early. He'd spent the past hour or so on the terrace with his laptop, researching Jason Streng. Most of what came up was already known to him. Streng was a young-looking thirty-four; his parents had come to the UK from Antigua. He had been a track athlete, and after making a series of commercials for Nike had completed a surprising transition into a main-stream movie actor, starring first in a wisecrack-heavy heist movie. It was popular with American audiences because it took place in a London that Londoners struggled to recog-nize. In the car, as they discussed the actor, Tim tried to conduct himself as if it was quite normal that from tomor-row Streng would be delivering lines he had scripted – admittedly only a few, but even so.

'I liked it when he did the, erm, what do you call them?'

'BAFTAs?' Miles guessed.

'No. You know.' Ruth was wearing a black polo-neck dress, covering up the cluster of freckles around her sternum; her hair hung loose down her back. What do you call it?'

'Comedy?' Tim joined in. 'Theatre?'

'The peregrine falcons. He did a series on them, for the Discovery Channel.'

'Sounds thrilling,' said Raf.

'I can't believe we're actually going to meet him tonight,' said Jo from the front seat. Christian had gone on ahead to greet the star in person before the event began. 'I bet I'm going to get all giggly and schoolgirl-ish.'

'I bet you will, too,' muttered Ruth, out of her earshot, and Tim tried to deflect a twinge of jealousy by taking in the scene out of the window. They were heading downtown. Billboards nestled on rooftops and yelled from the roadsides. Dirham prices were plastered over images of sports cars; phone networks and satellite-TV suppliers jostled for motorists' attention. There were huge posters bearing nothing but the beaky, affable face of Sheikh Mohammed. But mostly, what was advertised was the city itself. BE PART OF SOMETHING EXCEPTIONAL, urged a billboard for a chalk-white, tree-dotted residential development. DUBAI PEARL: WHERE THE FUTURE IS TODAY.

Tim remembered Christian saying that he had shares in this place. The Ropers had shares, by all accounts, in half of

Dubai. Their actual home was on the Palm, a collection of millionaires' rows sitting on a promontory which had been created from scratch by dredging earth from the seabed. This sort of wealth was distant from Tim's experience, and it was probably vulgar to be attracted to it even in the superficial, touristy way he was. All the same, as the forest of super-high-rise buildings sprung up alongside them, against a sky that was still midday blue as evening approached, Tim could feel himself falling for the story all great cities tried to tell: that this place in some way belonged to him.

The Sands Mall, the venue for the launch, was still open when they arrived, but in a final-hour lull which felt terminal. A handful of Emirati were browsing the windows of designer shops with fronts done out in imitation brickwork; outside a branch of a British menswear shop stood a Royal Mail postbox. The convention hall was reached via a glass lift which scooped them like a giant's hand onto a mezzanine. Here, behind a series of doors guarded by increasingly muscular men, was the action. Plinths shimmered with the familiar photos of WorldWise projects. Bradley Ford Richards – who had arrived early, with Christian – was consulting a set of cue cards and mouthing key phrases to himself. About forty or fifty people were being served cocktails by staff who seemed to turn their eyes away each time a drink was taken. In a corner, next to a determined-looking blonde who must be his agent, sat Jason Streng. He wore a dark suit and was, from a marginal glance, at least as handsome as he seemed in the movies. He sat sipping Coke Zero – the drink also favoured by director Bradley – and listening impassively as his agent described his wishes to Raf.

'Jason doesn't want to read the stuff you sent. He'll just speak briefly and then you can introduce him to three people, as per the contract.'

Tim glanced around to see if anyone else had heard this and was enjoying the absurdity, but even Ruth barely flinched. This would make a great story when he was home, Tim thought – in fact, he sensed he was going to have a whole pile of them. He moved away and took a cocktail from a tray, thanking its bearer warmly in an attempt at bridge-building which immediately sounded crass to his own ears. He found himself on the fringe of a group of British people, women teetering on heels and stocky-necked men, one of whom was telling a story.

'You remember? Rich and Poor Dinner?'

There were several affirmative chuckles and the story-teller went on. 'So the whole thing is, you paid, like, 300 dirhams a head, but the catch was, half the people got a massive meal, booze, all lovely; and the other half just had to eat bread and drink water. You know. To show how unfair it is, the rich–poor divide, that stuff.'

'Tell them what happened,' goaded one of the narrator's friends.

'So, Colin. He pays his 300, right, plus he brings some bird, a Thai bird. Then Christian Roper stands up and does his speech about how, if you're pissed off that you're not eating properly tonight, imagine how it feels to be one of the dispossessed. And it sinks in with nearly everyone. But Colin's been drinking all day and he shouts out: I'm not paying all that money to eat this shit! Christian says, that's the whole point! This dinner is about injustice! Colin says, for 300 dirhams I'd rather eat in a restaurant and worry about injustice another time! And then – and this is where it gets tasty—'

But the end was cut off by the Fixer. He had placed a firm hand on the storyteller's shoulder and the gesture seemed to drain the man of his energy.

'Ladies and gentlemen,' said the Fixer, 'it is time for the main event.'

And indeed the lights were going down. There was some tipsy 'ooh'ing. Christian Roper went to the microphone, greeted by applause and a couple of ribald-sounding shouts. Christian gave a précis of the speech from the previous night: that this campaign would help to counter inequality by getting people to donate; that they were lucky to have Jason Streng; that they hoped to reach twenty million people with the ad and its digital spin-offs. Tim felt intoxicated by the scale of things once more. 'And now,' Christian concluded, 'I'd like you to welcome a commercial director who needs no introduction: Bradley Ford Richards.'

The American had to slant the mic downwards to compensate for the difference in height. Sweat glinted on his nose as he placed his cue cards on the lectern with a slowness Tim found difficult to bear.

'What is a commercial?' he began at last.

'It's an advert, you silly sod,' muttered Raf.

'A commercial is a piece of work which asks for a reaction,' Bradley said in answer to his own question. 'So, it's a conversation between its creators and the audience. A negotiation.'

'Jesus Christ,' said Raf loudly.

Tim felt Jo's arm on his sleeve. 'Come on,' she whispered.

He stared at her. 'What?'

'Come on.'

Nobody glanced their way as he followed her, the two of them like fish skimming through a tank. Bradley Ford Richards' voice went on in the background: '. . . awareness. Awareness is everything.' With a dexterity Tim admired even through his general alarm, Jo picked up two cocktails from a tray and shoved open the door with her other hand.

They were out on a balcony in the thick air. Below was a muted drone of car horns. The moon looked as thin as a fingernail, the stars washed out by constellations of neon-lit windows.

'I'm sorry.' Jo took a generous mouthful of her cocktail and passed the other to Tim. 'I've heard Christian beat the drum so many times.'

'Do you not . . .?' Tim wasn't sure what he meant to ask. 'I mean . . .'

'I'm sorry. I sound like such a brat.'

'You don't.'

'I haven't had anyone to talk to for ages.'

'You can talk to me. Obviously.'

'It's just,' said Jo, 'everyone in there claps Christian on the back, and I just get looked at like a Jumeirah Jane, and—'

'Like a . . .?'

'It's what they call these wives here who are all, you know. Personal trainer, credit card, manicure, pedicure, the car, the rest of it. Everything but the husband; the husband's out earning it, and then playing golf and going for drinks with Roger and the rest of the *boys from work*.' She put an icy emphasis on these words. Tim coughed tactfully.

'But you're not like that . . . I mean, you two . . .'

'No, I'm not like that,' said Jo. 'I'm the comms director; I basically run 80 per cent of WorldWise. I always have. When the kids were growing up, right from when I was twenty-three, twenty-four, Christian was never there. He was always in the Central African Republic or Bangladesh. I was changing nappies, watching my body fall to pieces, *and* organizing press events in the evenings.' Her eyes were glittering. 'But he was the famous face, so he was the hero. He got the OBE, was in *Time* magazine. And I was the "behind every great man" . . .'

She tailed off and drank down the rest of her cocktail.

'So how do you two . . .?'

'How's the marriage?' Jo smiled as if it was an old-fashioned question. 'There's actually nothing wrong with it. I mean, we love each other. But, I don't know. That's not always enough, is it?'

Applause was faintly audible from inside. Tim wondered if they really ought to be out here on their own. He started to say something, and at the same time Jo caught hold of his wrist and pulled him to her with calm efficiency, and the two of them were kissing, the taste of the drink and the utter assurance of her lips striking him in the same moment. 'You smell so nice,' she muttered. 'I wanted you to stay, earlier. To come in the hot tub with me.'

'I . . .' said Tim.

She sighed and reached down for his belt, and then to Tim's utter exhilaration and alarm her hand was on his cock, and something made him stagger away.

Jo looked questioningly at him. Tim felt red and confused;

he removed his glasses as if that would help, rubbed them and put them back on.

'Isn't this a bit risky?'

'We can go somewhere.'

'Also . . .' Tim stared at the ground. 'Also, I don't know that it's right.'

'You don't think I should be the judge of that?' Jo had folded her arms across her chest.

'I mean . . .' Tim backtracked. 'I mean, I'm sorry, I . . .'

'Fine,' said Jo, and she walked past him to open the fire door. Tim made an impulsive reach for her hand. But she pulled away and he followed her at a distance of ten paces back into the room, where Jason Streng had just finished speaking and was being photographed, the camera-flashes bursting around him like fireworks.

The party didn't go on long: filming would start early tomorrow. In the car, everyone chatted about how friendly Streng had been, how paranoid his agent was. Jo did not look at Tim as they all parted at the Centrepiece. Tim, Bradley and Ruth, whose chalets neighboured one another, walked back together.

'What an asshole,' said Bradley, out of nowhere, as they were on the point of exchanging goodnights.

'Raf?' said Ruth.

'He is a *grade-A* asshole.' Bradley rubbed the side of his face.

'Are you OK, Tim?' Ruth asked. 'You're quiet.'

He longed to tell her about Jo, but the tale did him little credit, and could get back to Christian. Besides, he suspected that Bradley had seen him leave during the speech, and that this had contributed to Bradley's mood. All in all Tim felt he had made enough of a mess of things for one night, and it was better to quit here than risk some new mishap.

In his chalet the air-conditioning felt maliciously cold. He was getting used to the fact that it was seemingly able to override his commands. He got quickly into bed, pressing the button to draw the drapes across and leaving a pile of clothes folded in their usual place. After lying there for a few minutes he decided to get a bottle of Chardonnay from the minibar, and after two glasses he accepted it was inevitable he would think about Jo, about the brief moments she touched him. Then things felt a little better; he began to develop the sense that the slate might be wiped clean by morning, when the infallible sun came up again. He tried to usher himself to sleep by thinking about the riddle of the dollar, but he was not even sure he could remember the question correctly.

5: OLD TOWN

The chalets all had horsehair welcome mats, and sturdy locks on the doors even though they were opened by electronic card. Presumably this was to encourage the feeling of cosy domesticity, of the 'village'. And indeed Tim did already feel at home, despite the unmissable foreignness of the setting that was waiting outside, emphasized by the call to prayer that came wafting along the beach. It was hard to tell whether the muezzin's mournful cry was a recording or not; it had a slightly distorted quality, but that might just be the distance. The man drew out each breath over a fistful of alternating high and low notes. Distracted by this, Tim jumped as Ashraf made his way in. He was wheeling a trolley topped with a huge ice bucket, in which bottles bumped gently together like limbs in a pool.

'Good morning, Mr Callaghan.' The pronunciation was perfect now; he must have practised it. 'It looks as if you are leaving the chalet. May I go ahead and service it?'

'Yes . . . yes, of course,' said Tim, who had been about to use the bathroom but felt this was now inappropriate.

'Thank you, sir.' Ashraf went on to solicit permission to re-stock the minibar; then his eyes took on a watery, almost sentimental look. 'I also wanted to say thank you for giving me such a great report on the questionnaire.'

'Oh. You're welcome.'

'This is very good news for me. My superiors keep a record. In March I was the most overrated employee.'

'Sorry? Oh – the highest-rated employee.'

'Yes, sir.'

As he wove along the signposted paths, past crouching maintenance men and the early-shift holidaymakers – mostly the very young and very old – Tim found himself wondering how Ashraf could know about the result of the satisfaction questionnaire. Surely these things were anonymous? What if he had been critical?

He turned his thoughts instead to the day's filming. He'd seen the fruits of his work committed to camera before, but never with such a large production team, nor with a major star involved. All the same, as he looked at the day's shooting schedule, the main thing that jumped out was the absence of Jo's name. She and Christian were not on set today; they wanted to focus on the publicity and allow everyone some 'creative space'. Tim thought of the kiss with an uneasy sense that it could not really have happened, or that more should have happened; in any case, the way it *had* played out felt like the worst outcome. He wondered briefly how Jo remembered it – what was on her mind at that moment – and then made a half-hearted vow not to think of it again.

In today's filming plan Jason would walk down a street naked, in a location downtown, though any actual nudity would be supplied by a body double. Tomorrow they were heading to a golf club to capture him 'flying'. On the remaining three days they would then return to either or both locations depending on what else needed to be 'covered off'. It seemed a fairly forgiving schedule to Tim, but as he joined the group waiting outside the Centrepiece, Raf was already irate about the fact that their transport had yet to arrive.

'As soon as you start dealing with fucking locals,' he muttered, hooking his Aviator shades irritably onto his shirt so that he could make out the screen of his phone.

Tim took a long slug from a bottle of water. He had read on Google that it was advisable to drink more than you thought necessary, since dehydration happened quickly and was hard to detect. Ruth was tying back her chaotic hair in a number of ways, none of them very successful. She swiped the water bottle playfully from Tim. 'It's too hot already.'

'It's going to be proper warm, as the Geordies say,' observed the Fixer.

'How do you know about Geordies?' Tim couldn't resist asking.

'Family in South Shields,' said the Fixer. He was not able to elaborate on this surprising statement, because Raf intervened with an ill-tempered enquiry about speeding up the transport company. Like a Disney character summoning a magical protector, the Fixer appeared to click his fingers and whistle; almost immediately a large people-carrier rolled up in front of the Centrepiece, and the team piled in. Raf seemed about to ask why the Fixer couldn't have done this all along, but then thought better of it.

Tim was sandwiched between Ruth and Bradley, who was consulting a tiny notebook. As far as Tim could make out, he was reading the same few sentences again and again, occasionally mouthing a word. Raf took a phone call and once more loudly notified someone, whom he addressed as 'babe', that he was in Dubai. Almost as soon as they had set off, the driver apparently went the wrong way; the Fixer addressed him sharply in Arabic and the man, muttering, swung the car around on a dual carriageway, into a chorus of horns. Tim felt everything inside him tense with the certainty of a crash, and caught his breath again when the driver stopped abruptly at the next lights, having given every impression of intending to go right through them.

'This guy's a bit . . .' Tim murmured to Ruth.

'Not by Dubai standards. The whole place is like bumper cars.'

'Have you been before?'

'I worked here on, erm, on another thing for WorldWise, a few years back. Even stayed in the same place. It's changed a lot, though. Like, a thousand new buildings. That kind of thing.'

There were construction sites everywhere as they came down the Sheikh Zayed Road. Men in orange jumpsuits sat in neat rows, like children in a school assembly, while others swarmed around diggers.

'It'd be quicker if they all worked at the same time,' Raf suggested.

'They are on a break,' the Fixer explained. 'But there's nowhere really to go, so they just sit down.'

At the merging of lanes they got caught in a knot of traffic, and for several minutes crawled along beneath advertising hoardings for the new resort Atlantis. Tim wondered why they would name it after a place that had famously sunk, but this was displaced from his thoughts by a pressing need to urinate.

'Is it far?' he asked.

'Not far at all,' said the Fixer, 'but in Dubai you don't measure distance by distance. You measure it by cars.'

They pulled up eventually at the end of a pedestrianized

boulevard with a hamlet of construction vehicles, where dozens of men in overalls swarmed over walkways of scaffolding. As he looked up, Tim could see what all the work was in aid of: a thin building was poking from a sheath of scaffolding, like a present halfway out of its wrapping paper. The sun bounced fiercely off its glass exterior and cranes stood around like bodyguards.

'This is Burj Dubai,' said the Fixer, 'or will be. The world's tallest building by far.'

'What are they going to use it for?'

The Fixer wrinkled his nose. 'They haven't worked that out yet.'

Tim consulted his call-sheet. 'Aren't we meant to be in the Old Town?'

The Fixer removed his Panama hat and used it for a sweeping gesture. 'Old Town is the name of this entire development: the Burj Dubai, Dubai Mall and all these apartments. They're doing the apartments in the style of ancient Arabian architecture and that new mall over there is going to be done out like a souk.' Sitar music, from invisible speakers, was playing from the direction the Fixer indicated; the mall looked finished, though there was nobody about.

'But is there actually an old town? There must be.'

'There's the creek. That's the real old area. But it's not what you'd call a town. What they're recreating here didn't really exist in the first place.' The Fixer beckoned them along with him. 'Anyway. It's getting older the longer we stay here. Let's go.'

There was a large WorldWise trailer at one corner of the boulevard, where the mismatched-looking team of Miles and Bradley began to set up cameras. Tim made straight for the trailer, where there was the familiar purr of air-con and a table had been set out with snacks and drinks. The hiss of water pipes invited him through a side-door. A sticker on the cistern asked HOW ARE THESE FACILITIES? Tim had just started to piss, with a warming sense of deferred gratification, when from another room there came the clack of heels and a pair of voices he recognized: Jason Streng and his agent.

'I shouldn't be in that situation,' Streng was saying. 'Yeah? It's too dangerous.'

'I know, I know,' said the agent, and Tim had the terrible realization that he was in the star's trailer, not one for general use as he'd assumed. 'It won't happen again.'

'It *can't* happen again,' Streng insisted. His accent was of the kind that evolved in British stars after time spent in Hollywood: London-polished vowels, a lazy West Coast drag. 'There's too much at stake, Elaine.'

Tim tried to imagine what he'd do if someone tried the door. There would be little option but to admit he'd overheard a conversation that was clearly private and in some way volatile. His heart had speeded up. He lowered the toilet lid soundlessly and sat down, trying to steady his breath. A few moments passed like this; Streng insisted that 'it should be written into the fucking contract' and his agent promised that it had been, her voice pleading for his trust. Then the two of them went out, Elaine's heels sounding on the steps. Tim experienced a gratitude so strong it almost made him light-headed. He waited thirty seconds, slipped out, and immediately ducked around the back of the trailer for fear of being spotted.

But nobody was looking. Miles and Bradley were having an animated discussion about exactly where the main camera would be positioned. Miles gestured up at the sun and shook his head; Bradley looked through the lens, deliberating. Raf was glancing peevishly at his watch. Tim wandered over to the set, puzzling over what Jason and his agent could possibly have been talking about.

Tim's time on previous ads had taught him that things always took longer than expected, and that the more people were on hand to help, the slower things were. Even so, he was surprised that on the first morning of the million-pound shoot, absolutely nothing was committed to film.

The crew were in constant motion, especially Ruth.

Under orders from Raf she fetched bottle after bottle of Welsh mineral water; she placated Elaine the agent, who asked repeatedly for a parasol in case Jason needed to stand in the sun. Ruth was also the main conduit between Raf and the surprising number of extra staff who materialized as the morning went on: a make-up lady with fingernails as pink as cake icing, a continuity advisor, and a fashionably stubbled photographer in a khaki jacket. But none of this effort added up to any tangible result, at least as far as Tim could tell. The time was spent in moving cameras, marking and re-marking spots for people to stand in, and then changing the plan and doing it all over again. Bradley in his baseball cap gestured expansively and gave nasal instructions; Miles, his quiff drooping in the heat, hefted cameras like an overgrown boy moving model cars. Jason occasionally appeared, watched for a moment – inscrutable behind his dark glasses – and then retired to his trailer again. This phoney war continued from half past nine until well after noon.

At around twelve thirty Jason was brought out of his trailer and put into position. Six extras were lined up by Bradley, ready to walk past in the background. Miles peeked through his lens and gave a thumbs-up.

'Are we good to go?' asked Bradley.

But Ruth was surveying the parade of extras with hands

clasped to her sides. 'How old are you?' she asked a youth in a grubby football shirt with large, melancholy brown eyes.

'Sixteen, miss.'

'We can't have . . . he can't be here.' Ruth appealed to Raf. 'We don't have insurance for under-eighteens.'

'Please, miss,' said the extra, taking a step towards Ruth; he was half a foot taller than her. 'I want to work very much. My family needs it.'

Ruth gnawed her fingers. 'I'm sure. Look. The thing is, we're not allowed to . . .'

'Please, miss,' began the young man again. 'I am the only one in the family who can find work. I—'

'I can't do it!' Ruth said in a voice that came vulnerably close to a yell. The Fixer intervened, placing a firm hand on the would-be extra's wrist and leading him away, responding as the boy protested in a language Tim did not understand.

At five to one, they were finally ready for the first shot. Jason was brought out once more, Ruth holding a parasol over him. Bradley peered for a final time through the lens and then retreated to a spot of shade. Miles, looking as hot as a joint of meat on a barbecue, lifted the viewfinder to his eye and gave a nod.

'OK,' said Bradley. 'Speed. Camera. And—'

'Hang on,' said Jason, 'what am I saying?'

'It's here,' said Tim, seizing a chance to be useful. 'I've got the script—'

'Just tell him,' Elaine cut in. 'Tell him and he'll give it to you.'

Tim had slogged for days over this small amount of writing; he found he was able to recite it without difficulty. 'What if I told you an unbelievable fact: by 2016, 99 per cent of the world's wealth will be owned by 1 per cent of us. But when you see something with your own eyes, you have to believe the unbelievable.'

'All right, Rain Man,' said Raf.

'OK,' said Bradley, 'let's go with that.'

'If I can just jump in,' said the continuity advisor, who was a small ponytailed lady, so quiet until now that Tim had forgotten she was there. 'I wonder if "unbelievable fact" might actually make people think it's literally not true.'

Tim felt called upon to defend not so much his work as the company's aims. 'Well, the thing is, the whole concept here is "believe the unbelievable". We're deliberately flagging up how unbelievable it is.'

'I see that,' said the ponytailed lady. 'I just wonder about softening that message.'

'I don't think there's much point in the message,' Tim said, 'if we soften it. The point is how obscene the poverty is. Surely.'

Tim's point won the day, but more time had been swallowed up. It was two minutes to one by the time Jason had been briefed. Again Bradley ran them through speed-camera-action. Jason walked into the shot. Tim felt a clutch of excitement, in spite – or because – of all the hassle.

'What if I told you—' Jason began, gesturing chummily at the camera.

'Sorry, sorry,' said the sound man, motioning over his shoulder. The noise of drilling was blaring from the construction site. The sound man slipped off his headphones. Miles straightened up from his camera, hands on hips; Bradley clutched his forehead.

'OK. Everyone back to first positions.'

'And that's lunch,' Ruth said, looking at her watch.

This announcement animated the team as nothing had so far today. The crew members left their posts at once, as if they were elves who had been working under some spell from which they were now released. Elaine the agent ushered Jason Streng away before anyone could speak to him. Raf and Bradley, locked in conversation, went immediately to the front of the line. The rest of the crew formed a hierarchy which Tim hoped he was imagining, the photographer and continuity advisor and Fixer all ghosting in front of local crew members as though they were not there. Tim caught up with Ruth.

'Do you want to sit down? I'll get you something.'

Ruth seemed amused. '*I'm* not the charity case here.'

'No, no.' Tim took off his glasses. 'I'm just . . .'

'This is what I'm used to,' said Ruth, 'it's the job. But it is damn hot. I'm sweating like, what do you call it?'

'Er . . . like a . . . pig?'

'Sweating like a bitch.' Ruth dried her hands on her top. 'I think that's, that's the, that's the phrase I want. Ah, shit.'

As she bent to collect a tray, she had dropped her big, impractical bag, and the floor of the catering truck swam with her possessions: coins and receipts, a lip-salve, a disposable camera, a chunky historical novel, a faded photo of a boy of about eleven. Tim got down to help, in the process losing his glasses, which slid off his face. The two of them scooped up their things, shuffling out of the way of the queue as it bustled past. Ruth smiled in acknowledgement.

'You're a good man.'

'Is it always this chaotic?' asked Tim.

'That thing with the kid was horrible.' She paused. 'I mean, it was exceptional. But everything is exceptional in some ways, because the thing with this shoot is that there's a problem with—'

They sucked in the conversation as Raf approached, wearing his characteristic expression of contempt and impatience. 'Ruthie.'

'It's Ruth, thanks.'

'Ruth. I do apologize. Can I just ask why the fuck we have a location where they're going to interrupt us every ten minutes with construction work?'

'I'm sorry.' Ruth spread her arms in penitence. 'I was led to believe this was the old town, not the middle of the city.'

Raf shook his head and went away. Tim tried to think of something to say to Ruth, but she had already left in the opposite direction. He collected a tray of food and sat down on a table next to a man who introduced himself as Ian. He was of similar build to Jason Streng, and had the same skin-tone, but was less good-looking: Tim realized that this was the body double.

'Looking forward to it?' asked Tim, not sure what to say.

'Totally,' said Ian. 'Nice gig to get. Been out here before?'

'I haven't, actually,' said Tim.

'Came out a couple of years ago,' said the double. 'Stayed with friends, they work for Deutsche Bank here, you know? They have this thing called bubble parties, on a Friday. Friday is the holy day here or whatever. So all the Brits and the Aussies and that, they get together and go from hotel to hotel, having these brunches. But brunches is basically a code word for just getting rat-arsed.'

'Sounds great,' said Tim.

'And you should see Christmas, mate, seriously. Everyone

gets together and starts at nine in the morning and just gets completely shit-faced.'

'Fun!' said Tim.

'And New Year. Honestly, mate. Everyone gets, and I'm not exaggerating here—'

Tim wedged a new question into the smallest of gaps. 'So have you done . . . have you done this sort of thing before?'

'Naked stuff? Speciality, mate. Done scenes in *Hollyoaks*, done a couple of ads, all nude. So gradually, what you want is to become someone who's seen as being able to do stuff with clothes on. Cross that border into clothed gigs.

'I used to be a personal trainer,' he added. 'Still do a bit of it, if you ever need.'

Ian reached into his trouser pocket for a business card – something that would not be possible, Tim supposed, when he was actually working. Tim was relieved when Ruth came to say that lunch was over.

Almost as soon as the afternoon's work began, Raf became anxious about the time all over again, and he expressed that anxiety by snapping at anybody nearby. As Miles and Bradley began their pageant of setting and re-setting cameras, muttering to one another and glancing up at the sun whose very existence they seemingly took exception to, Raf made an ever greater show of checking his watch and sighing. He reminded Tim of a teenager forced to stay at a tiresome family event.

'We're not just standing here with our dicks out,' Miles explained, with the placid air of someone who had spent years disregarding requests to go faster. 'We don't get this right, it's going to look silly.'

They only had the location until four o'clock, apparently, and it was already two. The Fixer and Ruth went off to negotiate an extension to the time, though in the former's opinion this was 'as likely as snow falling'. He said it with one of his grins, which did little to improve Raf's mood. Tim wondered why, if time was so pressing, they hadn't begun earlier in the day, and why a whole hour had been deemed necessary for lunch when it was served right there on the set. He tried to make himself useful by taking on the menial tasks that would have been Ruth's. He fetched water for crew members and took a taxi receipt from an extra, to pass on to Ruth when she returned. Eventually, as Jason emerged from his trailer, the agent close at hand, Tim was given the job of holding a parasol over the star. It was the closest he had been to Streng, if you didn't count the time spent as an accidental intruder in his bathroom. As they walked towards the set, it felt a little like being one of the people who carried the Pope's sedan chair. Tim stared down at the ground, trying to observe the dictum that nobody could talk directly to Jason, but to his surprise Jason broke the silence.

'You one of the runners, mate?'

'No. I'm the – I'm the creative on this ad. Tim Callaghan.'

'Good to meet you.' Jason Streng reached out to shake his hand. The agent glanced at Tim for a second as if to appraise his suitability for this honour.

'There aren't any runners,' she said, wryly, 'because of everything we talked about.'

'Oh yeah,' said Jason Streng, and fell into a pensive silence. Tim wanted to know what this meant, and the question made him think again of the conversation he'd overheard. But there was no time for riddles just at the moment: the shot was finally ready. Elaine, the agent, reminded Jason of the line he needed to say; the make-up lady fiddled briefly and ineffect-ually with his face; the continuity expert made some remarks about 'integrity' which, meaning nothing at all, were quickly forgotten.

'Speed, camera. And action,' called Bradley.

'So,' Jason began, snapping from apathy into a kind of camera-intimacy Tim admired. 'What if I told you an un-believable fact: by 2016—'

'Wait, wait,' shouted Miles. 'Ah, too late. Someone in shot.'

It was Ruth, trudging back from her assignment. Her T-shirt was damp with sweat, and her body language suggested someone who had been standing up for several days rather than hours. As Miles called out, she looked up and realized she had wandered into the camera's view, but it was too late: they would have to start again.

'Sorry.'

'Jesus Christ, Ruth.' Raf put his hands on his hips. He appeared to be chewing gum. 'Did you at least get us some more time?'

'It's not possible,' said Ruth.

'Another fine mess,' murmured Miles, with as little sense of grievance as ever.

'The Fixer's still there, negotiating; he's offered them, erm, what do you call it, what do you call them?'

'Bribes?' Tim suggested helpfully.

'U2,' said Ruth. 'He's offered box tickets to U2. But it's still ongoing.'

'Oh, I like U2,' said the sound man. 'I mean, not so much the newer stuff, but . . .'

'*Joshua Tree*,' agreed Miles. 'Classic. Cast-iron classic. I saw them—'

'Fucking hell,' Raf burst out. 'We've got two hours here. We've got virtually nothing in the bag because nobody seems to be able to do their fucking job. Now I've got crew members walking into shot. I mean, is it amateur hour?'

'We're not just pissing about,' said Miles, still calm. 'We don't get these angles right, we're not going to get anywhere.'

'We're not getting anywhere as it is,' said Raf.

'I am making a commercial here!'

This was almost a scream, and it had come from the previously taciturn Bradley. The sound of his raised voice sent an immediate hush around the set; they could hear the faint cry of another muezzin, and the thrumming of the construction vehicles.

'This is not a high-school project!' Bradley continued, taking off his baseball cap; sweat glistened on his bare forehead. 'This is millions of dollars! I am going to get every shot right if we are here till Thanksgiving!'

'I don't know when Thanksgiving is,' Raf began, 'but—'

'Maybe you should look it up, buddy!' Bradley cried, and although this made little sense as a comeback, the director began to walk away as if he had conclusively won the argument. The whole crew watched as Bradley left the set, heading for the WorldWise trailer. His stride was so small, and the gesture so melodramatic, that he seemed certain to turn and come back with every step until the trailer door slammed behind him.

'That's a genuine tantrum,' said Ruth; she pronounced the last syllable of the adjective like 'wine'.

'Well, now I've seen fucking everything,' said Raf.

There was virtual silence; the continuous hum of activity around the fringes of the set had been stilled. Local crew members bowed their heads, as if frightened to be caught watching this scene. Miles and the sound man looked at one another in bafflement. Tim could see that nobody knew what to do.

'I'll go after him,' he heard himself say.

It was only as he reached the trailer that he wondered why exactly he'd volunteered for this, but it wasn't the first time. He had always been a peacemaker. He'd once resolved a dispute over a taxi between a drunk Rod and a total stranger, which would otherwise have led to a fist-fight. People sometimes saw it as a kind of saintliness, not grasping that Tim's loathing of arguments was so ingrained that his motive in cutting them off was largely self-preservation.

Bradley could be doing anything, Tim thought as he walked in: could be ready to harm somebody, could be headbutting the wall. But in fact the director was sitting completely still in a chair, his little notebook held in trembling hands. He looked at Tim with what seemed like gratitude.

'Are you OK?'

There was a pause.

'All I need,' said Bradley, 'is the space to work. I am not a guy who asks for a lot on set. I need people to be patient. That's all.'

'I think it's just that everyone is under strain,' said Tim.

'Well, sure, because . . .' said Bradley, and then his voice seemed to shake a little. 'I am just trying to make a commercial here.'

'I know,' said Tim, touching Bradley lightly on the shoulder. This seemed to galvanize Bradley; he rose from his seat. 'It's just all a bit frantic,' Tim added, sounding very English to his own ears. 'And, you know, the heat.'

'Sure,' said Bradley. 'I appreciate you coming out here,' he went on, as though Tim had made a long journey to speak to him. 'OK. We can do this. We can do this. I'll be back in a moment.'

Tim wondered, as he walked back to the set, whether Bradley's flash of emotion – so extreme, and so quickly dispersed – could possibly be about the argument alone, or whether there was something he was not being told here. He had an increasing awareness of comments not quite made, sentences left to tail off; something unspoken, anyhow. But for now, he had done well. He sensed the relief of the group as he conveyed the news that Bradley would soon be back. And as the filming recommenced, with a sense of purpose that suggested at least a semi-reconciliation between the combatants, Tim could feel people looking at him with a certain admiration which he had to admit he enjoyed.

The traffic was heavy on the way back to the Village, and Tim pressed his face close to the window to admire the jagged cityscape that hemmed them in. The sky was still an unbroken blue and the heat was still in the air, pressing on the car like a giant pair of hands; inside, though, the air-conditioning made it too cold if anything, and Ruth – who had looked ready to burst into flames earlier – now wrapped a cardigan around her shoulders.

Work had proceeded well for the final couple of hours, and at the wrap there were tentative handshakes between the main players. But although there was no urgency about their return to the resort, the car's laborious progress quickly sent Raf into another of his scathing moods.

'This city's fucked up,' he said, to nobody in particular.

'I'm sorry it is continuing to fall short of your standards,' said the Fixer, for the first time introducing a gentle mordancy into his voice.

'You know what I read? The residential areas, they don't have proper street names, people's addresses are just things like D23 or whatever. So if you try and find someone's house, you can't. There was a kid choked to death last year, just choked on a piece of food. The ambulance literally couldn't find his house and the parents were there going "left . . . right at the end . . . what number are you on now?" for twenty minutes. Asking him for landmarks he could see, and there weren't any. And by the time they got there it was too late. I swear to God, I pissed myself; it should be in a sitcom or something.'

'They have updated the system since then,' said the Fixer quietly.

Raf began to sing 'Where the Streets Have No Name'. Tim felt Ruth tense a little next to him.

'You didn't seem like a fan of U2 earlier,' said Tim. He was trying to reproach Raf for the tastelessness of the joke in a light-hearted way, but Raf turned in the front seat and looked at him.

'Know what I saw earlier? I saw you going into Jason Streng's trailer. What the fuck?'

Tim swallowed. 'Yes, I—'

'Has it not been made clear that we don't do that?'

'I was trying to find a toilet.'

'Well, maybe next time ask a grown-up for help,' said Raf.

Tim felt his cheeks smart. The car was quiet. He could hear his heartbeat in his ears. Tim wasn't even technically working under Raf, as the crew members were. He was here as the creator of the project; his status ought to be equal to Raf's at least. He glanced around the car, receiving a grimace of sympathy from Ruth, but nobody else caught his eye. Bradley was staring down at his notebook. Miles was toying with his hair, trying to restore life to his wilted quiff. The Fixer's eyes were out of the window, focused on the hectic road rushing by and the minarets and advertising hoardings, the dry expanses of earth where workmen and machines teemed; his thoughts could have been anywhere.

6: NOBODY

Christian Roper tapped a glass so energetically that Tim feared it might break. Then he went back to marvelling, through a mounting fuzz of drunkenness, that all these near-strangers were in his room. But – perhaps because of the length of the day, or the general intensity of all his impressions so far – nobody felt like a stranger. It was already hard to believe he hadn't known these people a week ago.

'To all of you who've worked your arses off today. Rest assured all the blood, sweat and tears have been worth it.'

When they got to the Village, the team had joined the Ropers at another beachside restaurant, where a private area was cordoned off for them. Tim had worried that Jo might act with hostility towards him, while semi-consciously allowing himself the hope that something of last night's spark might remain. In the event, neither had occurred: Jo had given him a polite smile before returning to her conversation. Then, when dinner was over, she'd wandered off to smoke with Raf; Tim could see them on the beach, under the gaze of the Burj Al Arab, which was lit in gradated shades of red so it looked like a paint chart. There was an ease, and a complicity about them which gave rise to an envy in Tim he felt foolish acknowledging.

Perhaps it was this, or perhaps his medium level of intoxication, which made Tim put himself forward when somebody suggested a final nightcap before bed. The sun's eventual retreat had left a sky divided once more into blue and maroon, like the layers of a pudding, before this was pulled away to reveal a broad splash of stars over the sea. Everyone but Jason and his agent was still there; filming was not due to begin until lunchtime the next day, because of the golf club's opening hours.

'We can't go to my chalet,' said Bradley, vehemently enough that he had to explain: 'It's, it's kind of a mess in there right now.'

'Does Ashraf not clean yours?' asked Tim, surprised. 'He's cleaned mine to within an inch of its life.'

'All back to Tim's, then!' cried Raf, and Tim found himself agreeing, rising to what he perceived as some sort of challenge.

For the first few minutes it was very odd to have them all there: the famous Christian Roper on his knees, methodically emptying the minibar; Ruth adjusting the air-con with a confidence Tim himself couldn't boast; the Fixer deflecting enquiries about where he lived, what else he did with his time. But, after all, this was not really Tim's chalet; it was nobody's, and especially so given that Ashraf had restored it to the perfect neutrality it had worn before Tim came. His clothes were folded out of sight; his bathroom was showroom-spotless. As a green-shirted girl arrived with more booze, leaving a satisfaction questionnaire, Tim allowed perfect, giddy ease to wash over him.

Music was on at a low level; people went out to the terrace and came back in. A double-bleep of his watch informed him that midnight had passed by the time Raf, beer in hand, proposed a game.

'Got an idea. Remember what the man here – remember what he made us do? One fact about ourselves?' He looked around the group. 'All right, so leaving aside all the bullshit. How about we do one *actual* fact. One thing that's *actually* interesting. A story. A secret.'

Tim looked at Raf, thinking how drunk he sounded; the eye contact was fateful. Raf reached across and slapped him chummily. 'Come on, mein host. Why don't you start?'

Once more, Tim's brain told him that he was being put on trial, tested by the group's alpha male; but with the insulation of booze and the rather dreamlike atmosphere, his brain added that he was equal to it, that he should say what the hell he liked.

'OK. My brother – me and my brother Rod were best mates. We did everything together. Had all the same jokes. He got me into bars, took me to festivals. All that stuff. And then, last few years, we just drifted apart. He went into the City. Then abroad. And then lost touch with everyone. We don't even know what he does now. Something with money. We hear from him maybe once a year. And I miss him.'

Tim wasn't sure he had expressed himself clearly, but the story seemed to be well received. Christian Roper, his shirt-sleeves rolled up as if he might start digging a well there and then, cleared his throat.

'I'll tell you my secret,' said Christian. 'I think it's fucking disgusting I have what I have, and you all have what you do. Poverty – this whole thing – is not a hobby for me.'

'That's hardly a secret, dear,' said Jo, stubbing out a cigarette in one of Tim's mugs.

'No,' said Christian, 'but still I don't think people fully realize that—'

'I'll stop you there,' Raf cut in, with a rudeness that surprised Tim, even given the producer's recent history. 'Do you not think that all this, this charity shit, in the end it's a bottomless pit?'

'What exactly do you mean?' asked Christian. Tim,

groping through his mind's blur, tried to divine whether Christian seemed angry, but his sense of nuance had been depleted. He could only register the physical fact that Ruth had gone into the bedroom and was now lying on the bed, facing upwards, still seemingly awake.

'I just, I don't know,' said Raf. 'This thing about it all being our responsibility. I get what you're doing. But I just think, the world is pretty screwed.' He gestured at the coffee table as if it were a map of the doomed planet. 'There's . . . Africa. You've got the Middle East. There's disease, kids dying every-where.' He had the drunken orator's habit of stopping for unpredictable periods and then rebooting just as someone else was about to get in. 'There's been charity appeals for-ever. They keep doing it. But people keep . . . you know. My point is, I'm not sorry I live in a nice part of the world. I'm not going to apologize for that. Kids dying somewhere else. The world's not fair, is my point. It never will be. Not our fault.'

Christian Roper spread his hands and said: 'Well, we must agree to differ.'

A few seconds elapsed before Miles began to tell a story about sitting on a snail and claiming that his younger sister had done it, so successfully that she herself still believed it was the truth over thirty years later. Everyone laughed; the awkwardness engendered by the previous conversation was soon gone. At least, as far as Tim could make out, it was; but he could feel reality pixelating, objects swimming into shapes pleasantly removed from their normal precision.

Later – when it was important – Tim struggled to remember in what order people had left. Bradley was first to go, he was almost sure, and the Fixer absented himself without ceremony or comment shortly afterwards. Then Christian, Jo and Raf left in a three, going out onto the terrace and never reappearing. Tim felt more distanced than ever from the moments of intimacy with Jo, but this manifested itself less as a thought than as an acidic twist of the stomach, and he forced his mind to alight somewhere else.

A strange sort of emptiness had descended. The rugs bore the imprints of recent human engagement, the air still hissed with past conversation. But two people remained. Miles had fashioned a bed out of two giant burgundy cushions and was lying in the middle of the lounge, face down and fully dressed, already snoring like a giant in a fairytale. Meanwhile, Ruth was still in Tim's bedroom. He rose from the couch to speak to her, and a warning shot from brain to guts made him sink back down.

'I'm going to go to sleep right here,' she said, 'unless you make me move.'

'No, I'll be fine on the couch.'

'You can come in. I mean, this bed's big enough for—'

'Honestly.'

He wasn't sure whether he was snubbing her, and it bothered him that he was too drunk to judge. But after everything that had happened with Jo, it felt advisable not to take any chances. In any case, Ruth was almost asleep, and soon Tim would be too.

He stood and took one more look at the scene: this new friend of his passing out on the bed, another crash-landed on the floor; the mess of bottles and drafted-in ashtrays. There was the dense mucky smell in the air of a just-finished party, an aroma that in only a few hours would provoke nauseous regret. There was no way of getting around that, Tim knew. It was half past two here, half eleven at home. He texted Pete. *It's mental here!* The phone wrote 'metal' instead of 'mental'; he sent this message by accident and was forced to issue another text as a correction. He stripped to his underwear and folded his clothes in a pile by the couch, which instantly proved as comfortable as the bed itself.

Sleep was reaching out for him, but when it came, it was of a brittle kind. Several times he found himself padding about in a hazy place he was used to, neither asleep nor really engaged with wakefulness. Once he tiptoed into the bathroom, flicked the wrong switch and accidentally filled the bedroom with light. Ruth stirred and muttered; Tim apologized. When he came out of the bathroom, she was awake, and he perched on the edge of the mattress. The bed-side clock said 04:15: he'd barely been asleep two hours.

'You, erm, get around a lot in the night, huh?' said Ruth.

They spoke for a few more minutes, Ruth with the covers pulled up over her shoulders. She invited him into the bed again, once more with an air of pragmatism – 'it makes sense' – but did not seem offended when he went back to the couch and curled up, as he always had in strange places, with his hands over his closed eyes.

The muezzin was calling outside and light was streaming in. Tim's bowels were nastily full and his head was aching with what felt like a sort of contempt for him. He checked the time; it was just after nine, though it felt as if he hadn't been asleep more than a few minutes. He hauled himself up from the sofa and registered two things: the door was open a little way, and Miles was no longer on the floor. Other than these details, everything was as it had been; Ruth was exactly where he'd left her, head buried in the pillows. All the same, something was wrong, but again it was impossible to say, with hindsight, whether he knew this as he gathered up his jeans – a mixed shower of pennies and dirhams clattering out of the pockets – and stepped out in search of fresh air.

The air, for a start, was not fresh. The new day had the kind of heat that the previous ones had only hinted at. There was an unpleasant frankness about the light. Outside this group of chalets, the perpetual good times of the Village would be starting up once more: the deckchairs set out in the same patterns, the shiny cocktail shakers perched on bars, the swimming pools shimmering and blue, as welcoming as newly made beds.

Ashraf was the first person he saw: he was standing outside chalet number seven. Tim began a greeting, but it froze in his mouth. Ashraf was clutching the top of his head with both hands, as if about to wrench all the hair out in one grab. He was swaying like somebody with seasickness; he barely seemed to recognize Tim. The cleaning trolley was parked a little way away, forgotten about.

'Ashraf, are you all right?'

Wordlessly, the cleaner pointed at the open door of the chalet, and Tim felt his overfull insides churn with foreboding. Ashraf was taking huge, unsteady breaths; he did not seem able to speak. The idea of going any further gripped Tim with fear, but at the same time it seemed to become almost unavoidable.

Tim walked slowly into an entrance identical to his own, with the lounge on one side, the main bedroom on the other. He went into the bedroom. Raf Kavanagh's clothes were scattered by the side of the bed; his watch and phone had been placed neatly on one of the bedside tables. His radio-alarm clock showed a non-time, 8:88. Tim progressed to the en-suite bathroom, wiping his damp hands on his shirt. Out of habit he knocked on the door; there was no answer. Tim removed his glasses, replaced them, and pushed the door open.

In the centre of the bathroom was a hot tub and there lay Raf Kavanagh, resting limply against the porcelain tiles around the rim. His eyes were dull and unmoving and his mouth half open. There was no doubt at all that he was dead. Tim began to say something, but he realized – with a feeling unlike any he'd had in his life so far – that there was nobody there to talk to.

PART TWO

7: CLOSE-UP

They drove in the falling dark. Nobody spoke. The vehicle purred along the trunk of the Palm, encountering few other cars. It seemed as if the whole place was a track built for this one car to make this one trip. Tim thought he was probably feeling that way because he didn't want the journey to end. It was comfortable in this vehicle. There were bottles of Welsh spring water poking out of grooves in the armrests; there was the in-car laptop in sleek silver. Nothing bad could happen while they were in here.

The Ropers' place was at the top of a marble-white block presided over by security floodlights, which burst on as soon as the group got out of the vehicle, as if to accuse them of something. The Fixer gave a signal to a dark-suited man inside who waved his hand over a panel to part the automatic doors. A brass plate above the desk welcomed them to NIRVANA APARTMENTS. The air-con exhaled. The concierge was almost asleep. The pinging sound made by the lift to announce their floor was the loudest thing anyone had heard for half an hour.

They heard a chain being pulled across, a sequence of bolts and locks being manipulated, before the door opened. Jo Roper was wearing a man's shirt, the sleeves rolled up; her hair was tied back, and there were pronounced circles around her eyes. Tim was ashamed to find himself reconnecting with something of what he had felt for her before.

In the entrance hall, the artful illumination – angled uplighters, ceiling bulbs – only emphasized how white and washed out they all were. There was something about their collective exhaustion that made him feel welded to everyone there. They had all suffered a loss together: the loss not just of a person, but of the assurance that the world was in good order, that things could not suddenly turn to madness.

From the second Tim saw Raf's body, a train of events had sprung into being. As he watched hotel staff arrive and summon the police, as he stood numbly with the other crew members having the same minimal conversations over and over again, he had the persistent sense that none of it was anything more than a charade he was going along with. He was aware this was probably shock, and almost welcomed the instruction which came from police around an hour later: that they must all stay in their individual chalets until further notice. It was good to have orders, somehow. It made it feel as if someone understood what was going on.

There was no one in the office in London; it was still too early. But Pete was often up before seven because of a habit of pre-work bike rides, which he undertook as a sort of voluntary penance for spending most nights in the pub. 'What's up, mate?' he asked. 'Grafting it out by the pool, you lucky bugger? Do you remember if I used up all the pasta sauce the other night? It's just I could swear—'

'Someone's dead,' said Tim.

'What?'

'The producer of the ad is dead.' The line was remarkably clear, as if Pete were in the same room: it enhanced Tim's sense that he couldn't really be so far from home, and in this confounding situation. 'Ashraf . . . the guy who makes up the rooms . . . he found him.'

'Jesus Christ, mate. What happened?'

'No one knows yet. Well, I don't know.'

'Christ,' said Pete again, sounding alarmed and impressed. 'Keep me updated.'

'I will.'

'Stay safe, Tim, will you?'

A sentiment as raw as this had no normal place in his interactions with Pete, with any of his friends; Tim felt unnerved as the call ended. It hadn't really struck him until now that he might be anything other than safe. He switched on the giant TV after some negotiation with the bedside panel and watched it play a promotional clip. A woman was shopping in a shiny mall; then returning to the Village, her haul of bags being conveyed to her room by a smiling porter. When Tim did find the BBC's world news service, there was – of course – no mention of what he had seen. A news event had happened here, but the news itself didn't know yet. The feeling of reversed authority was peculiar. He sat on the edge of the bed, staring dumbly at the cycling images of events elsewhere in the world, until two policemen knocked on the door.

They wore olive shirts with a red trim, and dark green berets with the logo of a ship and a wreath of Arabic characters underneath. It was very strange to lead the two men into the space where all his guests had assembled last night and which was still shabby and sour-smelling despite Tim's dazed attempts to clean up. One policeman perched on the sofa; the other, much taller and clearly the natural leader of the two, was glancing about the place. Tim wondered if he was drawing some sort of unfavourable conclusion from the fact that lots of alcohol had obviously been drunk here. It was stupid to worry, though: Dubai was awash with Westerners' narcotics. He cleared his throat.

'Would you like water, or . . .?'

'No, no.' The short officer seemed almost tickled by the clumsy attempt at etiquette. 'We just wanted to ask you a few questions. You know, obviously, of the death of your friend.'

It sounded even stranger like this than when Tim had said it himself. This was partly because 'death' continued to seem such a lurid idea, and partly because he and Raf had not been friends; yet now he did feel the beginnings of horror at the notion the man had died.

'Can you describe how you became aware of what happened?'

'I came out and Ashraf – the, er, cleaner . . . anyway, he led me to Raf's chalet.'

'Where you found . . .?'

'He was lying in his hot tub, dead.'

'Was the door already open?' asked the tall policeman.

'Yes.'

As he recounted these events, all true, Tim inevitably came to feel more and more as if he was covering something up.

'Do they . . . do you think it was . . . that someone killed him?' Tim found himself asking.

In a cop drama, one of the police might have snapped back that they were the ones asking the questions. These policemen achieved the same result by ignoring him altogether. The shorter man, removing his beret, began to ask about the previous night. Who had been in Tim's chalet? What was drunk, and were other drugs used? With whom did Raf leave, and at what time?

Tim strained to answer these questions with as demonstrative an air of helpfulness as he could. The last one caused him difficulty, given his sketchy memories; he was forced to admit – gesturing at the minibar – that he had been drunk. There were no other drugs, he said emphatically, but again with a creeping and unpalatable sense that he really had no idea what had happened outside on the terrace.

The lanky policeman's mouth seemed to twist into a sceptical grin at the unhelpfulness of his responses, but they did not pursue any particular topic to the point of discomfort. They asked some general questions about the ad, Tim's role, his career. He tackled these, feeling a slight slackening of pressure. The two investigators then made a brief search of the place, thanked Tim and told him he was free to go, although he should not leave the UAE for the next forty-eight hours.

'Thank you very much,' he said, as if they were plumbers who'd just carried out repairs.

As soon as he was released from the interview, Tim felt he had to get out of the room. He wandered into the Village, where two different days were beginning. There was the crime scene, bizarre as it was inevitable: cops with buzzing walkie-talkies, yellow tape around the chalet Raf had returned to only twelve hours before. But a minute's walk up towards the Centrepiece, or down to the beach, and everything was much as usual. The music of the bars swirled, ever-present and unnoticed, like oxygen. Guests with their towels and designer-watch catalogues glanced briefly at the policed enclosure and went on their way. In the Centrepiece, staff fielded enquiries about dhow rides and falconry displays as if these were matters of the utmost importance.

What Tim wanted was to see someone else from the group, someone in this same, almost hallucinatory state. But it felt as if calling on Ruth, or Miles, or anyone might be seen as the act of someone looking to change a story. He felt as if anything he did, even now, might have some retrospectively incriminating aspect.

With no better plan, he headed up to Catering Planet and sat in a corner booth, browsing the long menu without enthusiasm. At other tables, smiling staff were doling out satisfaction questionnaires and whisking trays away almost before they were done with. A waitress came over twice to ask if she could help; he ordered a Coke out of some sense of obligation to her, and sat cradling it, sipping it like a whisky. It seemed almost vulgar to think of eating 'twice-glazed sticky ribs' or 'surf and turf' when there had been a death. A death: the word was familiar like a game-show host, not dark or massy enough for what had actually happened, the destruction of a human.

These thoughts were interrupted by a man in a neat black suit, who was waving a pack of cards at Tim.

'You would like to see something, sir? Take one card, any card you choose.'

Tim felt his reluctance struggle with the eagerness in the magician's eyes, and perhaps with a growing sense that he was not fully in control of events and might as well go along with them. He took the six of diamonds, reinserted it into the pack, and watched as the magician fanned the cards out, tapped them with a forefinger and asked Tim to check his shorts. The six of diamonds was tucked into the right-hand pocket. Believe the unbelievable, thought Tim wryly.

'You liked that close-up magic, sir?'

'Very good.'

Tim hoped he'd said this with enough finality that the magician would now move on to somebody else, but on the contrary, he seemed to take the praise as a commission and continued. He made the card appear under the tablecloth, behind his ear, behind the ear of a waitress. With each twist Tim wondered if he was meant to tip the man; whether he was paid by the restaurant or reliant on kindness. The con-juror ploughed on, regardless: he transported cards into wine-glasses, made them vanish altogether, sliced them up with a knife and repaired them by magic. He had Tim sign a card and it turned up beneath the sole of his shoe. Tim watched and applauded helplessly, reminded of a day at a fairground years ago when the carousel operator suffered a loss of consciousness and the whole group of riders was trapped in motion for more than forty minutes. As he was thinking that a similar fate awaited him here, Tim saw the Fixer appear in the doorway. The magician greeted him.

'You like magic, sir?'

'I do a little bit myself,' said the Fixer.

The magician gave a gnashing smile, which Tim recognized as a look of professional wariness: it was the same look his father's friends at the model village had given to a Disney animator who'd visited once. He offered the cards to the Fixer, who directed Tim to take one. It was the eight of clubs. The Fixer invited him to replace the card, took the pack and, in a rapier motion, drew back his arm and whipped the cards at the wall. Tim saw them flutter through the air like ticker-tape; a solitary card remained stuck on the wall by some invisible force. The Fixer told Tim to peel off the outlying card. He didn't need to check to know that it was the eight of clubs.

'How did you . . .?'

The Fixer flashed a luminous grin. 'It's practice.'

Tim began to object that this wasn't enough of an answer,

that the thing he'd seen was impossible, but the Fixer was bringing news. 'I have been sent by the Ropers to say that there is dinner at their place tonight, on the Palm. Cars will collect you at half past six.'

'How did you know I was here?' Tim couldn't help asking, but with no expectation of an answer. The Fixer left. The magician was on his haunches, picking up cards from the floor.

Now they assembled around an oak dining table. When they entered, there'd been a general milling around and inspection of the open-plan space, with its arsenal of gleaming white fittings at one end, and floor-to-ceiling windows offering a chunk of the ocean over a spacious balcony. The décor was sparse: blurry fashion prints of New York and London on wet nights, streaky tail-lights and lovers arm in arm. From the ceiling in the kitchen area dangled the cooking implements, all in a row like washing on a line, which Tim remembered from the Skype chat many weeks ago.

Christian brought in a series of heavy silver pots and a criss-cross of delicious cooking fumes invaded the air. Tim realized with a little guilt how hungry he was, and how much he wanted a glass of wine.

'Obviously,' said Christian, 'this is a terrible day. It's a terrible day. We didn't know what to do. We brought you here because it felt like we should all be together.'

'We wanted you to know you're not alone,' Jo added. The Ropers' eyes flitted momentarily onto one another. Christian Roper's hand crept across the table to meet his wife's. The shadow of stubble did a favour to his face; there was something impressive about him. About all of them, in fact, as Tim looked around. Ruth had pinned her hair back efficiently; Miles had washed his, and it was slicked back from his forehead in neat comb-strokes. Bradley was in a polo-neck cashmere sweater and had left the baseball cap behind. Their efforts to rise to events had painted them all with a certain small-scale nobility.

'No one is alone in this,' Christian Roper echoed. 'We have all had a horrendous shock. I know you'll be wanting to talk and to think and . . . whatever you need, this place is at your disposal. That's all I wanted to say.'

'It's not quite all,' said the Fixer.

'No, it's not quite all.' Christian glanced down into his drink and back at the group again: either he was struggling with the effort of addressing them, or else he was a good actor. Of course, thought Tim, both could be true. 'There is the question of what will happen now. With the ad. I know that it seems in bad taste to talk about it. But it would be weird not to.'

Tim found himself leaning forward in his seat.

'We obviously don't know what has happened,' said Christian. 'We only know one thing.' He seemed to scoop up the eyes of each individual listener as his gaze circled the table. 'We set out to do good. The good we can do is not changed by what happened today. But nobody has to stay here. You might want to go home and forget all this. We will respect that. We will totally respect that.'

In the quiet, Tim glanced around the table. Everyone was looking at their cutlery, or at their fingernails. It felt like he should want to go home, but that was not the same as wanting it for real. To leave now, quite apart from possibly bringing suspicion on himself, would mean wresting himself out of a drama he had only just been flung into, back to a prosaic normality. He imagined the approach to the Shoreditch offices, the rain, the quiet mechanical transactions of people and computers.

'I'll stay,' said Ruth, quietly.

'I'm easy,' said Miles Aldridge, hungrily eyeing one of the pots, which contained a whole chicken bathing in a cream-coloured jus. It struck Tim as a rather casual response, but then, it was hard to know what the form was at a moment like this.

'I'm not a guy who walks away from anything,' said Bradley, drawing himself up very straight in his chair, like a seal stretching towards a proffered fish. He folded his short, neat arms across his chest. 'We came here to do a job. That job is to raise awareness. And that is what Raf would want right now.'

As Tim looked diagonally across the table he could see Jo's fist driven hard against her mouth as if she were trying to force herself away from tears. He confronted the idea that this death was an awful thing, a great and impoverishing disaster, rather than just an unsettling event. He could imagine Raf's mother, perhaps a mother very much like his own, in a medium-sized house in Oxfordshire, going brightly to answer the phone and hearing ten seconds' worth of words which shattered everything around her.

'I agree,' Tim heard himself say. 'We should stay.'

Almost everyone ate with an initial diffidence giving way quickly to vigour. Only Jo pushed and picked at her food. When Christian opened a new bottle of wine, Tim put out his glass without more than a momentary consideration of the echoes produced by the sound: last night's drinking session, before the unthinkable happened.

After dinner they settled in the lounge, which was dominated by a framed print of Grand Central Station in the twenties, light slanting in thick diagonal stalks through the windows. There was a trio of leather sofas, a vast TV screen and a fireplace. At last the conversation went the way it had to.

'Have they said anything about, erm?' Ruth had picked up a glass paperweight and was eyeing it as if it might contain a clue. 'I mean, do they know . . .?'

'It'll be a few days for an autopsy result, obviously,' said Christian. 'But the preliminary signs are, he'd definitely taken something.'

'Well, we know he'd taken *something*. When had he not?' Jo scratched her nose. Tim resented the implied intimacy, and he felt stupid for having thought that something unique had happened between Jo and himself. Then he pulled himself up with a silent shame that he was thinking that way at a time like this.

'So they don't think anyone . . . that anyone . . .?' Bradley began.

'That someone killed him,' Ruth said, in a mock-helpful tone.

'There's no way they could possibly say, at this point,' said Christian.

'There'll be reporters here,' Jo began. 'There'll obviously be talk about—'

'They won't find anything,' Christian cut her off. 'What are they going to find? They'll just show up and stick their bloody noses in.'

'I mean, there's no way anyone would have wanted to kill him,' said Tim, as usual a little surprised to be speaking out loud, 'even though, even though he was . . .'

'An aerosol,' said Ruth.

'Aerosol?'

'*Ass*hole,' Ruth clarified, with an effort.

There was a little nervous laughter, and a pause before Jo spoke, inching forward on the sofa where she sat next to her husband. 'Pretty bad taste that, wouldn't you say?'

'Speaking ill of the dead,' muttered Miles.

'I'm just saying what everyone thought,' said Ruth. Tim admired, and was a little appalled by, her courage. 'None of us liked him. If it was about someone not liking him, we . . . anyone could have killed him.'

'Sure, but people don't . . . you don't murder a guy because he's a pain in the ass on set,' Bradley objected. 'I'm not a guy that likes people to be rude, but you don't murder someone for being rude.'

'That's my point,' said Ruth. 'You don't. There has to be more to it than some grudge.'

'No one here would have, clearly,' said Christian, 'and everything that can be done is being done. So I don't know that we should be torturing ourselves over it. Who wants coffee?'

Over coffee and then an expensive-looking bottle of port,

the conversation veered away from the death. It was extremely odd, Tim thought at first, that this could keep happening: that for long minutes at a time, the group was capable of not discussing an event whose importance over-powered any other possible topic. But perhaps this was the result of an inevitable circuit-breaking mechanism: per-haps the subject was too heavy to be kept in the air all the time. Also – and again it was strange how quickly the brain accepted this – there was still a job to be done. There would be no filming tomorrow, Christian said, because of the amount of paperwork that needed doing.

'And because it wouldn't be appropriate, of course,' Jo said, her voice tight. 'It wouldn't be right to go straight back to it.'

'Of course,' Christian conceded; but he did not seem to feel it was inappropriate to resume talking about the mechanics of restarting the project. 'Seriously, back home, we'd be screwed now for two weeks. In Dubai, things just happen faster. When I first came over, I couldn't get used to it, the pace of it. Without Ali – I was phoning him ten times a day at first, wasn't I?'

'Dubai is a good place to win,' said the Fixer. 'That's what I told Mr Roper. A bad place to lose. A really, really bad place to lose.'

He gave one of his brilliant smiles, dusted with a certain

grisliness. Tim asked himself what game it was that Raf had lost, and to such a calamitous extent that he lost his life in the process. He felt the others must all be thinking versions of the same thought, though it was hard to say: Jo's face seemed deliberately angled away from his, and Miles was respectfully inspecting the aged port bottle from which Christian now poured himself an over-generous measure.

'And *I* said, OK, we'll win.' Christian swigged the port as if it were blackcurrant juice. 'We'll make kids the winners. Which we are.'

Nobody knew what to say to this. There was something impressive, even inspiring, in the sustained energy of the man; but also something odd or incongruous about the rhetoric, like watching a hyperactive TV show after a sombre news story.

In time, Jo spoke up to bring the evening to a close.

'We were thinking that if you wanted to stay here, anyone, all the rooms are made up. In case you didn't want to go back there, with everything.'

This had not occurred to Tim until now, but as soon as it was suggested he did indeed think how little he wanted to return to the Village, with its orderly lattice of pathways, its unctuous staff, the looming knowledge of Raf's death and the quiet way it was already becoming a non-fact.

'I'd like to stay,' he said.

'I bet you would!' Christian replied, looking across the room at Tim with a grin that triggered something momentary but unpleasant in Tim's innards, as if an ulcer had been brushed against. There was something in the way Christian looked between Tim and Jo that stirred dread inside him. Christian knew what had happened. Of course he did. Tim had done something inexcusable, and now this dramatic turn of events would flush the secret out.

All this jingled through him in the space of a few seconds, then Christian was patting him on the arm and showing him to a bedroom with such a complete lack of hostility that Tim could only think he had misread the moment. He was conscious that other members of the group were taking up the invitation to stay; as he crashed down gratefully on the double bed, he could hear them shuttling through the hall, doors opening and closing.

Glancing at his phone, he found a handful of replies had arrived to the various text bulletins he'd sent out during the afternoon. *You OK?* they asked. *Jesus, you OK? Thank you for LETTING ME KNOW*, wrote his mother, who had not mastered text messages, *and please Stay Safe.* There was an illicit pleasure in being in the middle of this exotic storm: assuming a certain survivor's status in the eyes of people back home. As he curled up in the bed, having folded his clothes into a pile, he clung on to this semi-comfort. It was better than thinking of what used to be Raf Kavanagh, a couple of miles away, stiff and lifeless in a steel locker, awaiting transportation to the heartbroken people whose son he had been.

When Tim opened his eyes, he had the familiar feeling that only a little time had gone by. He writhed onto one side and another, trying to make anything out in the pure dark.

The door swung open; he felt it rather than hearing it, felt the presence of somebody trying not to be heard. There were footsteps by the bed, and breathing. Someone might have been in Raf's room just like this. A bolt of terror went through Tim like electrical current and he heard his voice come out with unnatural harshness.

'What the fuck . . .?'

'Can I put the light on?'

It was Bradley. Tim exhaled slowly as a band of light fell onto the bed. Bradley raised his hands in apology.

'I've been sitting up. Suddenly everyone's in bed.'

Tim's composure was returning in uneven stabs. He shuffled to make room. 'You can sleep on the other side of this.'

'You're sure?' Bradley eased himself onto the bed. 'I guess I didn't really want to sleep alone tonight.'

'I know what you mean,' said Tim, and it sounded true as

he said it, though he was now struck by the slight strange-ness of this new arrangement. 'When you came in, I freaked out for a second.'

'It's horrible to think about it,' said Bradley. 'That some-one could have been in there waiting.'

It was a relief to discuss it so openly, but beyond Tim's imagination – or perhaps his will – to picture it. 'I don't understand who would have been. Or why. I mean, it would have had to be one of us. No one else has a smart card to get into Ocean Chalets.'

'This is a strange place,' said Bradley. Tim had the impres-sion that Bradley was turned towards him, though the light was off again now. 'They can say we're welcome as many times as they like. In the Village, I mean. But not everyone wants us here.'

'What do you mean?'

'I mean, Dubai is – this is still the Arab world.' Bradley's voice sounded slightly high-pitched without the accompany-ing graphic of his hairless face. 'They don't like our way of life. Americans, me and Ruth, are not popular here. We don't know this world. We don't really know what the rules are.'

Tim took a moment to digest this. 'But Raf isn't even American. Wasn't American.'

'No. I'm just saying. This kind of, uh, pleasuredome. The

drinking, the parties. All the excess. It's going to have consequences, right?'

Even now, with his eyes doing their best in the dark, Tim
could only make out the contours of Bradley's bare head, the
hint of his shoulder. 'But,' Tim objected, 'I mean, OK, yes, we
probably come across quite badly to some people here. But
not so badly that you'd – that anyone would sneak into Raf's
chalet, specifically his chalet, and kill him. It's insane.'

'You know what I read someplace?' Bradley said. 'People
kill for reasons that even they, themselves, aren't aware of.'

Tim reached up to remove his glasses and took a moment
to realize he wasn't wearing them. 'It's . . . surely it's much
more likely that he just overdosed on something. It sounds
like he had form with that sort of thing. It's pretty easy to
misjudge it, if you're pissed. I mean, he misjudged quite a lot
of things.'

'He sure did,' said Bradley, and gave a short, mirthless
laugh. 'Well, I know *I* didn't kill him.'

'I know I didn't, either,' Tim said, worrying immediately
that he had said this too hastily. But after all, it was true. Who
was left, then? Ruth and Miles, who'd slept in Tim's room –
though Miles hadn't been there in the morning. Christian
and Jo, who had both gone home. The Fixer; perhaps Streng
and his agent, although they were staying in another part of
the Village. No matter how much you ran through it in your

head, it felt ridiculous – like being at one of the murder-mystery parties his parents occasionally hosted in Devon. 'Who had motive?' he could hear his father asking the retired estate agents around the table, as tiramisu was served. 'Who had opportunity?' It was impossible to think of colleagues in this way, to apply it to a real situation. The only thing that made sense – or at least, that his brain felt up to – was to accept for the moment that there were things he could not know, could not understand.

There were a long, silent few minutes. Tim heard the hourly double-bleep from his watch. Very gently, Bradley's arm came across to rest on his chest.

Tim opened his eyes. There was no sound, no other movement; Tim couldn't even tell if he was asleep. He lay where he was and listened to Bradley's even breathing.

After a few more minutes he thought he heard a voice raised in another room, and a hasty shushing from someone else. He felt a yearning to be in his own bed at home, instead of this enforced physical contact with a man he barely knew, in a room too dark to see, in a millionaire's mansion – a millionaire whose wife he had kissed – twenty-four hours after someone had died in the night. Only this time yester-day, the unfamiliarity of everything had seemed so attractive.

He was almost certain now that Bradley was asleep, and he thought back over their conversation. It was true, he realized, that he knew virtually nothing about Dubai as anything more than a collection of well-presented ideas and images. He'd flown into the city like someone arriving at a theme park. It was easy not to ask questions about Dubai: that was part of its appeal. Now, however, certain questions could not be avoided.

8: THE WORLD

They had been allocated new rooms in another block of the Village, twelve floors up in a whitewashed building called Maritime Tower, which surrounded a swimming pool shaped like a four-leafed clover. From the window of Room 732 – well, really a whole glass wall, making him feel he could plunge straight down into the water – Tim could see a few couples idling on deckchairs, summoning green-shirts with a half-wave of the arm.

The day of inactivity before filming restarted would, even this time last week, have been a tempting prospect; now the empty hours took on a vaguely threatening shape in Tim's mind. He had no mental map of the city yet, and it did not seem a place that could be conquered with a sheer spirit of adventure, even if Tim had been that sort of visitor.

'How can I help you today, sir?' asked someone with SOPHIE on her badge, behind the Centrepiece desk.

'Is there . . . do you have any recommendations for things to do near here?'

'Sir, we can order you a car straight away.'

'But if I wanted to, to just stroll somewhere . . .'

Sophie's eyebrows suggested an artfully withheld scepticism. 'There is Zabeel Park.'

'And how do I walk there?'

'We can order you a car, sir.'

'Do you like shopping, sir?' The man at the terminal next to Sophie's had entered the conversation.

'Shopping?'

'Yes, sir, are you interested in Dubai's wealth of shopping options?'

His voice had the swish of someone eager to demonstrate mastery of a language. In Tim's peripheral vision, the promotional video played on forever: the golfer swung at a ball, the visitors marvelled at the ice models.

'Well, I—'

'You might be interested to visit the Mall of the Emirates. Very good designers and brands, good prices. Beautiful food court and ski slope.'

None of this appealed greatly to Tim, but staying here – among the oblivious holidaymakers, the never-disrupted rituals of leisure – was no more attractive. The floors of restaurants and saunas creaked above his head. At least, he thought, the mall would mean getting out.

'That sounds good,' he said.

The taxi driver was listening to a recording of an imam leading prayers, drumming his fingers appreciatively on the steering wheel. The Mall of the Emirates came into view, the ski slope tacked recklessly onto its side. Then it seemed to disappear again as the driver, his hand forced by a network of overpasses, swung them into a lane they weren't supposed to be in, and almost into the path of a Lamborghini. The other motorist blasted the horn and Tim started.

'First time in Dubai, sir?'

'It is, yes.'

'How are you liking it?'

'It's, er . . .'

'Very clean, sir, no?'

'Very clean,' Tim agreed.

'You throw even a small piece of litter out of the window, sir – a thousand-dirham fine. First time at Mall of the Emirates?'

'Yes.' The wail of prayer continued in the background; the air-con was almost icy. 'Is it . . . is it a good mall?'

'Very excellent mall. You like Paul Smith?'

'Paul . . .?'

'Paul Smith is in the mall, and Gucci also, sir. And Prada for your wife. It is – as you say in London – superb-duperb.'

Tim suppressed a grin. 'Have you been to London?'

'No, sir, but many English people come here. English people love to shop. Are you from London?'

'Originally from Devon.'

'Sorry, sir?'

'Yes,' Tim conceded, 'London.' He tried to think of something else to say. The approach to the drop-off point, outside the mall, took them down a spiral ramp, which the driver tackled like a funfair ride. 'So do you go shopping here?'

'Me?' The taxi driver flashed a white smile; Tim was reminded of the Fixer and of the recurring feeling that everyone here was in on a joke he didn't get. 'No. I drive the car.'

'But I mean, when you're not driving.'

'I am always driving the car, sir.'

A sign at the main entrance splashed red Xs across male and female forms. *Please dress modestly and appropriately.* Under a high, domed ceiling, lifts conveyed dark-clad women and sun-reddened tourists frictionlessly between floors, like nerves around a body. He looked in vain for a map. Everyone else seemed already to know where they were going: they moved as if following a plan.

There were no obvious store guides, and the whole mall was bigger than he'd first thought: what seemed like the central atrium gave way to a grander, roomier one, which in turn was the prelude to one bigger still. He followed signs to the ski slope, passing under a two-storey-high banner which trumpeted INTERNATIONAL BRANDS.

GIVENCHY

CALVIN KLEIN

DKNY

SELFRIDGES

NIKE

GUCCI

VICTORIA'S SECRET

CHANEL

LACOSTE

CLINIQUE

DIOR

HUGO BOSS

On and on went the list, running to forty or so names. There was nothing to explain whether these brands were already available here, or had outlets opening soon; the names were simply there, as if expressing some self-evident truth. English people love to shop, he thought. It was true; it must be. Dubai had not put up these palaces of commerce and leisure to amuse itself: they were there because foreigners – including the English – wanted them. The ski scope principally existed not because Emirati wanted to ski in the desert, but because Westerners wanted to go to a place so decadent that it was possible to ski in the desert.

All the same, there were some Emiratis here. At the entrance to the slope, a lady's eyes watched through the slit in her niqab as a worker in a polar-bear costume capered for the amusement of two kids. Two other women stood nearby, their forms obscured by the hijab; each held a bejewelled handbag. Nearby, a Filipino girl stood guard over a thicket of designer-label shopping bags. At a signal from the women, the maid picked up the bags and hung them on her arms, and began to usher the protesting boys away.

Through the viewing window Tim watched as tourists swished down the ski slope. A group in red jackets was attempting to mount a fake mountain range with an Alpine hut at the top. A fibreglass snowman looked on with a crooked grin. Tim bought a coffee – proudly brewed in the Italian tradition, according to the napkin – and listened to 'Santa Claus Is Coming to Town' oozing from the speakers. He thought briefly of Christmas at home: the afternoon lull, Miss Marple quietly solving an upper-class murder. The next song was 'Let It Snow'. Presumably the same CD played every day, including Christmas Day, regardless of the thirty-degree heat and the fact that Christmas was not part of the official calendar here. He finished the coffee and went on his way. 'Sir, Gucci?' someone asked; before he could process the question, a sample had been squirted onto his hand.

A banner advertised the EMIRATES PROPERTY EXPO. Waiters were circulating with silver trays; there were cardboard cut-outs of Big Ben, a Sydney Opera House, a rainforest and a Japanese temple. A woman in a turquoise sarong informed Tim that this was an exhibition for The World, the new group of man-made islands each resembling a country; he had an exciting opportunity to be part of something iconic.

'Are you interested in investing, sir?'

Tim gave her what he hoped was an inclusively self-deprecating smile. 'I rent my flat at the moment, so I'm not sure I can stretch to an island.'

The woman beamed, her eyes blank. 'So you are interested, sir?'

He regretted the stab at humour. 'I'm afraid not. Not for the moment.'

'You can sign up with my colleague over there for a boat tour of the islands which will further your interest.'

Tim wove his way through the waiters. He looked at the model Big Ben and thought about the model village jointly run by his father, which attracted a smattering of tourists.

Toy trains puffed around it on tracks; there were shin-high grocers' shops, a church, pubs with agonizingly hand-drawn signs the size of postage stamps. One morning a tiny wooden tennis player had been found keeled over on his hand-trimmed rectangle of grass; he was given a funeral by Mr Callaghan and his friends, in a ceremony which Tim and Rod were made to attend. 'That was really stupid,' said Rod, on the way home.

He swivelled to look at Tim, and Tim – wanting nothing more than to impress his brother – agreed: 'Yeah. The model village is stupid.' Mr Callaghan smiled sadly into the rear-view mirror, his long spine hunched over the steering wheel. 'Well, I'm sorry you chaps feel that way,' he said.

This was an unwelcome memory. It stirred an impression, perhaps sharpened by his distance from home, that his parents had never been much rewarded for their patience and effort, for the hundreds of days spent ferrying their sons around, providing whatever was needed, loving the boys in their undramatic way. Tim had never been disruptive or difficult, but he had made no secret of his glee at escaping to the big city, and he was lax about staying in touch; Rod had taken these traits quite a lot further.

The guilt that stole up on Tim was enough to make him think of buying his mother a present. It was awful, really, how little he had to do to thrill her, and yet how seldom he made the effort. He browsed windows until he saw a black lambswool coat on a mannequin. He remembered her owning something like this before. It was the sort of thing she would want to wear, but perhaps consider too fancy to buy herself, which was her attitude to most things; it looked just the right size, too. He went into the outlet with an encouraging sense that this trip to the mall was about to acquire a purpose, to yield a result. But when he asked about the jacket, the shop assistant – a bony and bright-eyed man – made an apologetic face.

'I'm sorry, sir, but this is the last one.'

'Is that a problem?'

'Yes, sir. I cannot sell you the jacket because then it will not be on display, and people will not know it is available.'

'But it won't be available,' said Tim. 'I will have bought it.'

The thin man nodded as if they were on the same side of the argument. 'Yes, sir. So we prefer to keep it on display.'

Tim could feel the pulse in the side of his neck. 'So, just to get this straight: you want to keep it here, so that people know it's available to buy. But if someone does try to buy it, you won't let them.'

'Yes, sir.' The man reached behind his counter for a flyer. 'Are you interested in the Shopping Festival?'

As he followed signs to the taxi rank, Tim felt as if the whole trip had happened to him, rather than being something he'd initiated. He passed a fish tank which had taken over a wall in a rash of blue: striped clownfish skittered in and out of each other's paths. Perhaps, he thought, the fish believed that they were in charge of the place, and the humans were there as ornamentation. A small boy came and banged on the glass, jabbering in Russian; he laughed as the fish turned tail. Outside, the heat clobbered Tim as he made his way to a taxi.

'Where your bags, sir?'

'I didn't buy anything.'

'You don't buy anything?'

'That's right.'

The driver swung them up the spiral ramp. Tim closed his eyes as they joined a line of traffic and came to rest there in a way that felt indefinite, like a stone dropped into a pond.

He found the panel to turn off the air-con and slid back the blinds. Outside, the weather had taken an inhospitable turn: the early-evening sky had curdled to a British grey. TV would dispel the gloom, Tim thought; it was for moments like this that you had a TV. Its opening offer was Beyoncé shaking her midriff into a grovelling bank of cameramen. A channel-change, and a scene appeared which initially struck him as some kind of visual joke. It was the Village. An American reporter was talking into a microphone, her eyes alight with the newshawk's relish for the regrettable.

'. . . said, in a statement, that the incident should remind Dubai visitors of the dangers of excessive consumption. This is Jacqui Nelson in Dubai, United Arab Emirates.'

Before Tim had adjusted to its being there, the picture of the Village was gone, supplanted by another story: a zig-zagging stocks-and-shares graphic, the caption MARKET FEARS GROW. He took off his glasses and started up his computer. His inbox was the usual crowd of bogus money-making schemes and needlessly protracted email exchanges from the office, but in the middle of it – sent only two hours ago – was a message which made him catch his breath.

> Bro,
> Heard about this murder on the net. Your name came up. You all right? I'm in Cuba. Give me a bell.
> Rod

There was a phone number, including so many digits that Tim was unsure where international and local codes began and ended. None of it mattered for now. What mattered was that this was as much as he'd heard from his brother in more than a year. He read the minimal message three times, as if by doing so he could somehow tease more out of it. He tried, out of some vague and superfluous sense of pride, to deny to himself that he was thrilled, and that the thrill was likely to disperse as soon as he tried to call the number and it failed to connect; or he left a message which was never returned; or he fell prey to any of the other ways in which his brother routinely disappointed him and all the other Callaghans. For now, Tim wouldn't try the number. He would simply enjoy the glow of this moment.

When he dragged himself away from re-reading the message, Facebook was the obvious next destination; if someone as remote as his brother could have heard about Raf's death, it must already be a major talking point online. Tim remembered that he and Raf had become 'friends' when the project began. This enabled him to go onto Raf's personal page, which was topped by a picture taken only hours before his death: an image of the producer in his Aviators, accompanied by the caption 'on set in Dubai – good times!'

Vacated by Raf himself, the page had become a shrine of remembrance. There was a stream of shocked comments, photos, testimonies. Raf was a beloved brother and son. He had paid for two strangers to get into Alton Towers when their credit card failed. He'd been a huge source of support to his brother-in-law, who was in a wheelchair. His stunned parents recalled a 'beautiful blond boy whom everyone loved', and who became a 'brilliant young man who made people laugh'. Raf Kavanagh's online identity was so comprehensive that it was hard to believe he no longer existed in physical form. This version of him was as real as the unpleasant man Tim had known. The more he read, in fact, the more he doubted that unpleasantness, even reproached himself for remembering things the way he did.

A link from Raf's page led to a newly established Facebook group: 'RIP Raphael Kavanagh'. It had 900 members already, and people had been posting as recently as ten minutes before.

This whole thing stinks 2 hell. I know it's not the time 2 talk about this. But truth will come out when there's an autopsy. Raf did not die because of some 'mistake'. Some1 knows something. WorldWise need 2 answer some questions.

Tim closed the page and sat at the desk wondering what 'questions' this commenter had in mind. He went onto WorldWise's site, but the content had been temporarily removed, replaced by a picture of Raf and a brief message outlining the tragic development. The first spatters of a surprise rainfall hit the windows, and although he had only recently got back, Tim felt a desire to be out.

In the lift there were two leathery businessmen, each

with a defiant arm around youthful Thai or Filipino companions. Tim looked away from the quartet, at a poster on the lift wall.

TEX-MEX NIGHT! BUFFALO BILL'S!
The authentic flavour of the Wild West.
Every Wednesday in Catering Planet, Centrepiece.
All food halal.

Rain was falling in skewering bursts, reminding Tim of the shower in the chalet, although the shower had been meant to remind him of rain. Around the swimming pool people were submitting to the changed weather with ill grace, rolling up towels, stuffing magazines and sun-cream into bags. They glanced up at the sky and exchanged grimaces as if a deal had been reneged upon.

In the Centrepiece – where he found himself heading, out of habit, out of some desire to ground himself – Tim saw Miles and Bradley; Miles in a heavy metal band's T-shirt and unwisely skimpy pair of swimming trunks, and Bradley, as ever, in his baseball cap with notebook in hand. Without actively intending to spy on the two of them, Tim crept close enough to hear Miles's usually benign voice raised in protest.

'It's taking the piss. It's absolutely taking the piss.'

MARK WATSON

'I agree,' Bradley said, 'but I don't see what we can do.'

'I didn't come all this way,' said Miles, 'to be treated like this.'

Treated like what? Tim wanted very much to ask. Who, or what, is taking the piss? But it was as if the questions externalized themselves without his permission: Miles and Bradley both swivelled at the same time and Tim was obliged to look as if he was surprised to see them.

'Just been to the water park,' said Miles, although Tim hadn't asked for this information. 'Checked it out.'

'Getting on with some work,' Bradley added, patting his notebook. 'You?'

'Oh, not doing anything really,' said Tim. 'Maybe see you later?'

'Maybe,' Bradley agreed, and the two of them departed, leaving Tim with an inescapable feeling of being left out. Both the overheard conversation, and their body language, had hinted strongly at something that Tim could not be privy to. He thought about the night he'd spent in odd proximity with Bradley, wondered briefly whether Miles and Bradley could be lovers, dismissed it as ludicrous, and then reinstated it because nothing, just now, was too strange to rule out.

He stepped outside, hoping to catch sight of his colleagues, but they could have gone in any of several directions.

The air was bracingly cool, at least in comparison with what he'd become used to; raindrops teased the back of his neck. Tim's eye caught a familiar figure scampering out of sight. He followed around the back of the building. It was Ashraf, an ill-fitting suit jacket over his green T-shirt. His large, white eyes were full of something that looked like fear.

'Mr Callaghan. How is your stay?'

'Hello, Ashraf. Heading home?'

Ashraf smiled faintly, as if unsure whether Tim was making fun of him.

'Home?'

'It's just – it looks as if you're on your way home.'

Ashraf tweaked unhappily at his moustache, which, now that his face was so solemn, had an odd, unhappy quality to it, like a disguise he was being forced to wear. 'I have been dismissed, Mr Callaghan.'

'Dismissed?'

'I am no longer working for the Village, taking effect immediately.'

Ashraf looked away and Tim had a horrible feeling that he might be about to weep.

'What?'

'My services have not been considered satisfactory,' said Ashraf.

'Is it because of the . . . the death?'

Ashraf looked at him in silence. It was obvious there was something he wanted to say. Tim felt desperate to pave over the gap in trust that made it impossible, but Ashraf was turning to go.

'Please take care, Mr Callaghan. I must go and catch a bus.'

Tim wondered how far beyond the Village, beyond the broad gate and the sentry-hut, Ashraf would have to go to find a bus stop. He wondered what would happen to him next. Every moment he spent wondering diminished his chances of ever finding out.

'Come back. Ashraf.' He was almost shouting. 'Let me give you money for a cab or something.'

'No, thank you, Mr Callaghan.'

'Ashraf . . .'

The small man seemed to weigh up some proposition hanging in the air between them. He mouthed a single word. There was a plosive, a B or a P. The fragment of sound died in the air.

'Sorry?'

Ashraf did not look back or stop walking.

'Ashraf? What did you say?'

Tim watched him disappear, the too-big jacket over bony shoulders, head down. It came as a nasty relief when his figure vanished into the nothingness that lay beyond the lantern-lit paths.

What was the word? It might have been 'balloon'. Or 'bidding'. It had been a punch to thin air. It was gone, and the man who spoke it was gone. Tim had the sensation that he was standing on the edge of a great dark something; that just beyond the solidity of the hotel was a void, a zero that could swallow a person.

He would have liked to call home – or call someone who wasn't here, at least – but it felt as if nothing he could say would make sense to them. He walked back down towards the beach, passing the bars and restaurants, where business was going on as usual. Tim had the thought that the resort was an organism, one that hardly needed its guests: if no one ever stayed there again, it would still start up again each morning.

He was almost at the beach – and still with no specific plan in mind – when he saw Ruth, deep in conversation with a bespectacled man. Tim had half decided not to disturb them when Ruth noticed him; it was a relief when she called his name.

'You look like you've seen, erm, seen a ghost.'

'I sort of have,' said Tim, and he described the encounter with Ashraf. The stranger, who had still not been introduced, called a waiter over and paid the bill; but when Tim finished the story, it turned out he had been listening.

'That's very interesting,' said the man, glancing down at his phone as if he planned to pick it up and tell someone straight away.

'This is Adam,' said Ruth. 'He's a journalist.'

'It would be good to catch up sometime,' said Adam, as if theirs was a well-established relationship. 'That's interesting, about the lackey getting sacked.'

'He wasn't a—' Tim began.

'He was the one who found the body, wasn't he?'

Tim already regretted having said anything in front of this man, who had clearly been pumping Ruth for information: perhaps with some success, judging by the number of beer bottles on the table.

'We're in the "Executive Compound", as it's enticingly called,' said Adam, touching Ruth on the shoulder with a surprising familiarity, 'but we'll mostly be in whichever bar stays open longest.'

'We?' asked Tim, as the reporter walked away, consulting his phone again. 'Who's we?'

'The journalists.' Ruth finished her beer and rapped the empty bottle down. 'Do you want . . .?'

'Yes. Definitely. Please.'

'We'll get two more of these, please. Or four, let's just say four.' Someone behind Tim went to execute the order. 'There's a whole load of them. Sky, CNN, the whole pack. This is what they do.'

'I suppose so. It's just weird to be . . . it doesn't feel quite real.'

'They're like a little gang,' said Ruth. 'There's the ones who go to war zones and are there drinking in Baghdad, their own little bars, the correspondents' club. "See you in Gaza in a couple of weeks." And then there's the ones like him, who just follow murders around.'

'Is it a murder? Did he talk about it being a murder?'

Ruth hesitated.

'Sorry,' said Tim. 'I'm feeling . . . I don't know what I'm meant to feel.'

'I know what you mean. I've been the same. I wanted to get a haircut but I feel like if I change my appearance, it's going to look like I'm hiding something. It's ridiculous.'

The beers were placed in front of them by a man who moved away so quickly that it was as if the transaction had something covert about it. Tim took a greedy chug from his, and was pleased to see Ruth do the same.

'But surely . . .' Tim began. 'I mean, surely it's more likely that it *wasn't* a – that there was nothing suspicious about the death.'

Ruth made a grab for a clump of her hair and sat there

with a fistful of it. 'I'm the main producer now. Obviously. I've been trying to make sense of Raf's files. I can't understand half of it. But I do get the impression a lot of stuff went on in the days before it happened.'

'What sort of stuff?'

In a gesture fuelled either by the beer or by his craving for humanity, for something to share, Tim reached out and put his hand on hers. Ruth's eyes changed, becoming wary.

'Sorry. I just wanted to say: I'm not going to tell anyone a word you say to me. I'm trustworthy.'

Ruth seemed to weigh this up, and nodded. 'Sure. Well, I know you didn't kill him, anyhow.'

He was halfway to savouring what seemed a compliment when he realized it wasn't meant that way: it was a statement of fact. 'Because you'd have heard me?'

'Right,' said Ruth. 'I *did* hear you. You got up in the night, like, ninety-two times, remember?'

'Oh. Yes.'

'You went to the bathroom and we had a whole conversation,' Ruth went on. Tim felt colour scatter across his face and settle there as she continued, smiling at him with a trace of indulgence. 'At the time of death they're giving – about three fifteen, three thirty – you were standing by my bed, kind of muttering and fumbling for the door handle or something. That's my main alibi. That's what I told Adam just then. And the cops.' She rolled her eyes. 'I guess you didn't give them the same story.'

'I already don't know what I said to them,' Tim muttered. 'Just by talking to them, I started to feel like I had secrets.'

'Sure, and everyone *does* have secrets. I have secrets. You have.' Tim nodded, wishing for a moment that he did have a life as complex as the one she was crediting him with. 'Most of the time you can live for years like that. And then you get caught up in something and it all comes out. That's what happens in murder mysteries, isn't it? And the reason it's in murder mysteries is because it's what genuinely does happen. Do you find it funny I say "genuine" like that?'

'Sorry. No. Was I smiling?'

'I accept my accent is a little weird. It's the part-Irish, part-American thing.'

'I like it.'

They smiled at each other. 'I'm glad you said that,' Tim admitted. 'It's stupid, but my only reference for all this *is* murder mysteries.'

'Well, they're everywhere,' Ruth said. 'Books in the airport. Every other TV show. Murder feels like, erm, it feels like fiction. You don't imagine – it's a cliché, but you don't imagine it happens, as a real thing, to people like yourself.'

Tim was onto his second beer; he felt emboldened. 'You

know – just on the subject of secrets – I heard Jason Streng having a strange conversation with his agent.'

Ruth listened as he described what had happened in the trailer. 'Right. See, that kind of thing is what I mean. Before the – the death, something already wasn't right.'

'Like what?'

'I don't know.' As Ruth shook her head, her hair fell about like foliage teased by wind. 'I don't *want* to know. I suspect Raf knew, and I am now in the post he previously held.' She finished off her beer, sucking the final drops with a practised pitilessness. 'It's – what's the phrase?'

'Er . . . A poisoned chalice?'

'No.'

'An unenviable position?'

'No. Keep them coming.'

'You want me just to list all the phrases that exist in English?'

'Well, do you have anything better to do? Are you going to solve the case?'

It was pleasant talking about the death this way, as if it was incidental to the business of them both sitting here; and it was good to feel the connection of a joke. 'All right. A headache? A nightmare?'

'No, no. Like, a more extreme phrase for something difficult.'

Tim rustled through his memory for phrases his mother might use on the phone, describing the dispute over the Faulkners painting their house a different shade from the rest of the street, or the book club's endless Tuesday-Wednesday-Tuesday fluctuations. There were no such whimsical expressions when she discussed Rod. There were just the slightly shrill assurances that he was 'up to all sorts of things', and, with each phone call that turned out not to be him, the half-hopeful octave rise of the voice followed by the return to earth. 'Oh, hello, Wendy. No, just . . . expecting someone else.' All of this made Tim realize he still hadn't called his parents since the news broke.

'Hell in a handcart?'

'No, no.'

'One of those things like the devil and the deep blue sea, or a rock and a—'

'Shit sandwich.' Ruth snapped her fingers. 'That's the one.'

'Ah, it's obvious. I should have got it.'

Each laugh left a little warm residue in the air, and soon more beer arrived. The impression intensified for Tim that all he had to do was stay in this seat, in the corner of this nearly empty restaurant replicating in roughly equal measures the cuisines of Italy and Vietnam, and everything would retain a comforting shape.

'It's been a weird day,' he said, trying to describe the mall: the rows of luxury items undisturbed by customers; the *Toy Story* figures, who were real-life versions of fictitious toys; the ski slope, and the world of cut-outs meant to represent The World, which itself was a model of the actual world they were sitting in. 'By the end of it, I started to feel like I was walking around in a sealed bubble.'

'Dubai can be like that. You feel like you're on a different planet from everyone. Then, when you want privacy, you can't get it.'

Tim thought he heard the flicker of a rebuke in this. 'Were you . . . did I interrupt anything, with that guy?'

Ruth looked straight at him. 'We were just talking.' The way she said it, he felt immediately that he ought not to have asked about it. 'How about you? Are you with anyone?'

'Me? No.'

Wanting to recapture the warmth of the conversation before he'd made what seemed like a faux pas, wanting to shed the burden of secrecy, Tim decided on a revelation. 'But there was – kind of an incident with Jo.'

This time the coolness of Ruth's stare was inescapable, and Tim's heart plunged. 'I don't want to hear this,' she said.

'It was nothing. Not really. Just a couple of moments, which—'

She was shaking her head. 'I don't think you should have done that. And I don't think you should be telling me.'

Tim felt heat rage through his face. 'Sorry.'

Ruth gestured helplessly at the heavens. 'Raf was messing around with her, you know that? Now he's dead. Jesus, Tim.'

'You think Raf was killed because . . .?'

'I don't think anything. I just think this isn't a good time to be talking about screwing the boss's wife.'

'I didn't—'

'OK. But even so.'

Ruth requested and paid the bill while Tim protested ineffectually. All at once they were getting to their feet and the bar itself was being cleared up, as if everyone had merely been waiting for the two of them to leave. A waiter thanked Tim for choosing them, and expressed the hope that they were having a good stay in Dubai.

They passed the occasional couple returning from one of the bars: a low laugh, a shared moment, hands meeting. Tim felt the returning gloom of non-intimacy, the sensation that other people there had bonds with one another, had a solid connection to this time and place which made less and less sense to him.

'I'm sorry I went for you,' said Ruth. 'I'm just . . . there's a little pressure on me right now.'

'I know,' said Tim, without feeling that he really did know.

'It was fun. See you at breakfast?'

He stood in the lobby of the Maritime Tower, wondering where Ruth was staying; he'd assumed that they were all staying in this building now. As the lift display went through a complicated light show – almost here, then vanished, then almost here again – he tried to reconstruct the conversation of the past hour. It felt oddly distant, already, and part of him wished he hadn't gone over to Ruth and the journalist at all.

The walls of the building were given over to a mock fresco of Neptune, rising angry-eyed from blue waters with his trident brandished. The painting rose all the way from ground level to the arched ceiling. It was at odds with the cloud-white lobby fittings, the don't-mind-me music which tinkled away on a forty-minute loop; the indifference to style was almost impressive. The cool air, humming through fans and filters, had come to seem like a natural element. There was nobody around as he slid his card into the door.

Tim's room, as usual, had been cleaned and tidied with an annihilating thoroughness. His discarded clothes were folded on the made-up bed, where there was also a satisfaction questionnaire. The blinds were closed; the TV was broadcasting to the empty room. Some drama set in a British vicarage, something his parents would watch, was on, subtitled in Arabic. A Home Counties churchman said that he could feel 'pure evil creeping through the parish'. Tim fished out a mini-bottle of wine, switched off the TV and curled up on the bed with the questionnaire.

> Out of 10 – where 1 is 'disagree exceptionally strongly' and 10 is 'agree exceptionally strongly' – how would you respond to these statements?
> My expectations of cleanliness have been met:
> By my room or suite
> By the Centrepiece
> By the washrooms and changing facilities across the site
>
> How did you hear about the Village? Please grade each of these propositions from 1 to 10, where 1 is 'this is utterly inaccurate' and 10 is 'this is absolutely accurate'.
> Regular visitor
> Internet travel site (please specify)
> Word of mouth e.g. recommendation from friend, family, colleague, business associate, religious leader
> Chance
>
> How likely are you to return to the Village in the next twelve months? Please rate the likelihood from 1 to 10, where 1 is 'it is inconceivable, even under the most desperate circumstances, that I will ever come to the Village again' and 10 is 'I have already booked my next stay and have signed up for a VILLAGE GOLD™ card to maximize . . .

When he woke up, Tim was upright and looking at nothing. He reached out for a wall, nearly toppling forwards in the effort, and shouted out in half-formed panic. Groping for the bedside panel, he got the TV on and, by its light, dug the card from his pocket. He walked to the door and slid the card into its slot and the room was flooded with light. There were dark smears of blood on his chest and arms.

'Jesus,' said Tim out loud, grasping that he'd had a nose-bleed – fluctuations in temperature, in air pressure, often did this to him – and had sleepwalked part-way to the bath-room to clean himself up. He washed off the blood, smiling wanly at his sheepish reflection. As he went back into the bedroom and his mind came to life like a restarted com-puter, the conversation with Ruth returned. It seemed suddenly that he'd been mad to pursue a flirtation with Jo, in a place like this where he manifestly didn't understand the rules. Then he thought of Ashraf disappearing into the night, discarded by the Village, again for reasons that were currently beyond Tim's grip.

He pressed the button to open the blinds, which ground across with a certain reluctance as if they too had been asleep. The stillness outside was glacial. Far below, the swimming pool lay a ghostly green, illuminated by floor-level spotlights. It was half past one in the morning. Tim thought of the cheap, sometimes alarmingly downtrodden hostels he'd visited in Australia, and then of the Callaghans' French campsites. In the former there had always been someone crashing back drunk. Even in the latter, where it was dead quiet at night, there had been the sense of life: the rustling of canvas, the cry of a child, the tangible nearness of other humans. This, thought Tim, was not that sort of place.

The memory of lying with Rod in the tent, trading whispered wisecracks over their parents' snores, made him want to call the number his brother had sent. Why not? he thought. Who cared what it would cost, what Rod would think? That was what normally stopped him from trying to get in touch, he realized: the fear of looking foolish, or needy. The current surroundings, the loneliness of this night, were enough to mute those concerns, at least for the moment. He heard a distant-sounding ringtone several times, and then, muffled but unmistakable and thrilling, his brother's voice.

'Yeah?'

'Rod? It's Tim.'

The pause that followed was so drawn out, Tim thought he had been disconnected. He pressed on. 'Are you in Cuba?'

'Yeah.' Rod's voice was becoming steadily more real. 'I was asleep.'

'Oh, sorry. I thought . . . I thought it'd be afternoon there, or something.'

'It is,' said Rod. 'I usually sleep in the afternoon.'

'Is that a Cuban thing? Like a siesta?'

'No,' Rod said, 'it's because I'm a lazy bastard.'

Tim heard himself laugh a little over-eagerly, but the ice-breaking effect felt genuine. 'What are you even doing in Cuba?'

'Kind of living in a commune. Don't worry,' he added, 'I'm fine. I'll come back soon.'

'To Britain?'

'Yeah. I just needed some time. The City – the financial stuff – it was killing me. So much bluffing. I got out just in time as well, I reckon, looking at the shitstorm that's coming.' Tim's spirits soared at the ease the conversation seemed to be acquiring. 'Anyway, so are you actually out in Dubai? Are you there, where it happened?'

'How did you know?' Tim – while still excited that his brother had made contact – couldn't avoid a flicker of anxiety at the idea that his name was somehow publicly connected with this death; so publicly that Rod could have happened upon the news.

'Someone sent me the link because they said it was your company. I Googled Vortex and it looks like you're working on it right now.'

142

'I came up with the . . . the concept for the ad, yes.' Tim felt himself trying to sound important. 'I came out here a couple of days ago. And out of nowhere this guy died.'

'And they don't know how?'

'No. Maybe some sort of overdose. Or maybe . . . maybe . . .'

'Christ.'

'Yeah.'

Tim was unsure how to maintain the momentum after this, and his brain reached for something more trivial. 'Hey, you'd be able to sort this out. Do you know this riddle about guys who check into a hotel – it's been bugging me – and they all pay—'

'The missing dollar,' said Rod. He sounded more and more like himself: the proud older brother, the arbiter; the person who had helped Tim arrange his books not alphabetically, but in ascending order of quality. 'Yeah. It's kind of a trick. They make you think everyone's paid nine dollars to the hotel, because they all got one back from their ten. But they haven't actually paid nine. Not really. It's . . . I'd need to show you on paper, but basically the whole riddle is an illusion.'

'When are you coming back? We'll go through it then.'

In the pause that followed, he wondered whether he had been too anxious to pin his brother down.

'Rod?'

The line had gone dead, this time. Tim redialled the number; it failed to produce a ringtone.

His heart was still beating quickly; after all, it had been a breakthrough of sorts. They'd spoken for the first time in more than a year. Rod had even mentioned coming home.

But as he climbed back into bed, with the bedside panel showing a time of two fifteen, qualms crept in alongside him once more. Their interaction already seemed implausible; the sudden cutting of the connection made it all the more so. Like the time he spent with Ruth, like the disturbing exchange with Ashraf, it seemed to have receded the instant it was over, replaced by the smooth nothingness of this room, high in a tower, in a complex where for the moment Tim felt like the only person alive. As sleep came hesitatingly once more, he tried to distract himself – as he had before – by thinking over the dollar riddle, but he wasn't sure he quite followed what Rod had said. His only clear impression was that he'd been trying to solve a mystery that did not really exist.

9: BLOCKS

The sun was pouring in and Tim had woken late, which came as something of a relief. Ruth had mentioned breakfast, he recalled, as the shower battered him with water. The idea provided a certain quaint comfort, conjuring up English country hotels like the one in Saddlecombe, where cutlery was clinked and menus fussed over at identical times each day. More of that sense of the humdrum, of a hotel's natural order, was what he needed. He didn't have Ruth's number, but perhaps he could get them to call her from the Centrepiece. He switched off the air-con, knowing it would somehow be on again when he returned.

At the desk, Tim had to wait, and his confidence in the plan quickly began to waver: Ruth would already be in the office, surely. Other people's days would be properly underway by now; he was out of joint with them. The cause of the delay was a man with a goatee and a shark-shaped inflatable under his arm, airing a grievance in Russian-patterned English.

'I am here two days, first my wife is at the property expo yesterday and she doesn't receive her free pass for shuttle, now I am wanting to go to Wild Wadi Water Park and I again don't have free pass.' He thumped his fist against the inflatable. 'I go all the way to Wild Wadi Water Park with shark and I am told I cannot come in, so I have spunked my time against the wall here.'

At last Tim got his opportunity; the receptionist named Sophie called him forward. Her hair was tied up in a net; her brown eyes stood out in a pale face. 'How may I help you in the Centrepiece today?'

Tim asked for Ruth's number, and Miles's as well, for good measure. Sophie pursed her lips in professional regret.

'Can you help me with some ID, sir?' asked Sophie.

'ID?'

'ID is a short way of saying "identification".'

'Yes, I understand,' said Tim. 'But . . .?'

'We cannot answer a query about a guest's location unless it comes from another guest who is a legitimate guest,' said Sophie.

'I've got my room key.'

'It needs to be legitimate ID, which includes a passport or driving licence,' said Sophie.

'I mean, I'm definitely a – a legitimate guest,' Tim pointed out. 'We spoke yesterday. About the mall.'

'We certainly did, sir, and remember to call 234 if there is anything else I can help you with.'

Tim took this as a sign that it was time to give up, and wandered away. Breakfast was still being served in Catering Planet. There were cereals, cold meats, fruits and yoghurts. Guests lined up, watching critically, as a lady in a green T-shirt cajoled batter into the shapes of pancakes and waffles; others went around the tables lifting silver lids and inspecting the insides of tureens as if suspicious the labels were lying to them. At one table, an attendant was doling out slices of toast as they emerged from the innards of a toaster so large and studded with slots and vents that it could have passed for a computer in an old sci-fi movie.

'Would I be able to get – just some bread and butter?' asked Tim.

'Our bread comes as toast, sir,' said the attendant.

'But could you just give me a couple of slices of bread before they go in the toaster?'

The attendant frowned. Tim had the sense of a great road-block between himself and the normal process of getting breakfast, and knew how easily his brain could inflate this into a block of a more serious kind. There's no need to over-analyse things, he told himself. He gathered up a bowl of mandarin slices, floating in juice, and was stopped by a hand on his shoulder. The Fixer was holding out a plate.

'Bread.'

Tim took it with a mumbled thank-you and began to weave through the tables, all laid out with white cloths and orchids, most unoccupied. Someone was on the stereo singing Madonna songs in a language other than English. There was no sign of Ruth. He walked on. No table was any different from any other, but somehow it seemed impossible to commit to one. He saw Bradley waving him over, with what seemed an unusually demonstrative energy. He was sitting with a tall glass of Coke crammed with ice cubes.

'I was trying to call you in your room,' said Bradley, 'but it wouldn't go through.'

'They won't even give *me* anyone's room number,' said Tim, intending it as the beginning of a humorous anecdote, but Bradley nodded rather sourly as if this only concerned some suspicion of his.

'What's up with that? I mean, what is up with that?'

Before Tim could ask what he meant, Bradley had shoved an annotated script in front of him. 'So, I have to talk to you about creative changes. You know, we are in kind of a difficult position here. There's going to be scrutiny. This guy, this journalist . . .'

'Adam?'

'I think he got into my room last night.'

'How?'

'Sweet-talking. Stealing a key. Who knows? I just see him skulking away and when I get back in my room, things have moved. I'm not a guy that likes things to move. I am not a guy that likes people to be in my room. Anyhow. My priority is to make sure we make the best commercial we can. That's the only thing I'm focusing on right now.'

Tim nodded. He wondered if this really was the only thing Bradley was focusing on: easier said than done, surely, to force out of your mind the unexplained death of a colleague and the logical prospect that anyone else could die just as suddenly. Tim studied Bradley's face. His shiny head rested on one palm like a pool ball awaiting the strike of a cue.

'OK,' Tim prompted, 'so . . .'

'So . . .' Bradley gestured at the first page of the script, marked with small, child-like handwriting. 'Right now, we have "by donating, you can send money straight to where it makes a difference". Christian's asked if we can change it so that we don't say "straight". It's a legal thing.'

Their eyes met. Tim felt that Bradley was preventing himself from saying something else.

'Some deep and meaningfuls going on over here!'

As if summoned by the mention of his name, Adam had appeared at their table. He looked tired in an oddly self-satisfied way. His white shirt-sleeves were rolled up like the sleeves of an overworked hack in a Fifties movie. The bags under his eyes communicated that he had stayed up all night reporting, speculating; talking about *them*.

'Not really. Just chatting about the script.'

'Still going ahead, are they?' asked the journalist.

'We sure are,' said Bradley.

Adam raised his eyebrows. 'Not easy for the Ropers. On top of everything.'

It was infuriating, the little innuendo, the hint of some bombshell discussed by the news-pack in their bar. Bradley held the journalist's stare with an amiable blankness. Adam said that he would love them and leave them.

'Well, that's half true,' Tim muttered.

'What?'

'Love us and leave us. Only half true.'

'I don't think I get your meaning,' said Bradley.

Tim took a deep breath.

'If you could just think a little about that change,' said Bradley, 'I just have to . . . uh, to visit my room.'

Even this banal statement seemed to carry some undertone Tim could not quite get at. Bradley folded up his script and tucked it inside his notebook with that meticulous slowness. They were all meeting in the WorldWise office, he added, at 1 p.m. for a briefing, before heading to the location.

Tim went back to Maritime Tower to gather his things before the briefing. As usual, there was almost nobody to be seen. He tried to make progress with the odd task Bradley had left him, of mulling over the 'creative change'. What am I meant to do with the request to drop the word 'straight', he asked himself, and why had this suddenly become important?

In the short time he'd been away, the room had undergone another comprehensive clean-up. The blinds had been closed, a kiwi fruit (Fruit of the Day) sliced in the fruit bowl, a laundry bag left in readiness. The invisible hands had left a fresh satisfaction questionnaire on the bed, stacked neatly on top of the one Tim had fallen asleep with last night.

Who were all these people who peered impassively into Tim's toilet bowl and removed stray foliage from his path? Did they get some sort of satisfaction from the work, or resent it? It was best not to think about it: that was how you managed in a place like this, and really – given the way the world was – how you got through anything.

Besides, Tim reminded himself: this is why we're here, isn't it? To tackle, in some way, the problem of inequality. That was the point of WorldWise and of Tim coming to Dubai to help them make this ad. He would try to keep that thought close to hand, today; it was easy, in the heat of all this, to forget that something real and important was happening.

Before going to the office, he thought he should call home: there had been several more texts from his mum, among the large number generated by the events. Like the one from the other night, they were laid out and capitalized with an unevenness Mrs Callaghan would never allow in her written correspondence, bespeaking a patient battle with the technology. He stood outside the Centrepiece. His mother answered, as always, on the third ring: efficient, but not so keen that people would think she had nothing better to do.

'Oh, Tim! I've been worrying about you so much!'

Her voice conjured not just their house, with its overwarm living room and the utilities humming contentedly in the kitchen, but the whole village. There was the old cinema with a screen only just bigger than the TV in Tim's room here, the ivy-conquered church whose graveyard contained the bones of the adulterous vicar. A clock mounted above the altar of the church said 'IT IS TIME TO SEEK THE LORD', but its hands had stopped moving years ago, giving the accidental impression that there were only two moments a day when the Lord was worth hunting for. There was a pair of better-than-nothing pubs where Mr Callaghan used to take Tim and Rod on Christmas Eve, to Tim's great pride and Rod's eventual disdain.

'I spoke to Rod.'

His mother caught her breath. He heard – across thousands of miles – her overwhelming relief at the proof of Rod's ongoing existence, and the almost immediate counterpunch of misery that she herself, who doted on him like no one else alive, had not received a call. 'Where . . .?'

'He's in Cuba.'

'Cuba,' repeated Linda Callaghan. 'Goodness me. What's he doing there?'

Tim tried to assess whether the word 'commune' would reassure her, or the opposite. 'He's just taking some time out. I'm going to speak to him again soon, so I'll get him to call you.'

'Thank you. Thank you, Tim.' She cleared her throat. 'So, how long are you going to be out there? It's been in all the papers here, the . . . you know, the death. It was in the *Telegraph*.' Although this was not the way she'd dreamed of it happening, Mrs Callaghan couldn't suppress a note of triumph at the milestone: 'I've been telling everyone: Tim's working on that show!'

'Well, ad. It's an ad. It—'

'I feel so sorry for the parents.'

'It's awful,' Tim agreed, irritation building inside him. It had to do with the tone of dinner-party gossip. He could imagine his mother talking like this at the book club. There would be people everywhere back home taking up the story like this, playing with it, putting it down: the discussion of the tragedy of no more significance in their day than a cup of coffee.

'The parents are saying it was foul play, you know. As I suppose you would. Whereas the – the Dubai people . . .'

The events were entertainment to everyone but those involved; they were no more real than the mocked-up rural murders the Callaghans would sit down to watch that Sunday evening.

'They're saying that it's all the fault of the Western world,' his mother went on. 'I think it's a bit of a cheek, personally. I mean, I *personally* would rather live in a country where a woman can walk down the—'

'I'd better – I'd better get back to work, Mum,' said Tim.

'Oh. Yes. All right. I'm sure you're busy.'

He felt the gut-guilt at her change of tone.

'You'll be careful out there, won't you? And will you come and see us as soon as you're back?'

'Of course I will.'

Outside the WorldWise sliding doors, Tim hesitated: an argument was in progress. He could hear Jo and Ruth's raised voices cutting across one another.

'So, right, we have the resources for *that*, but not for—?' he heard Ruth say, sarcastically.

'We have to do whatever he says,' Jo interrupted. 'And if you don't like that, Ruth . . .'

'Bit of trouble in paradise!' said a voice close to Tim, and Tim jumped, feeling he'd been caught snooping – though snooping on something that was, after all, his business. The jaunty platitude made him expect for a moment to see Adam, the reporter. But the man standing there had heavy black-rimmed glasses and a crew cut. He had come from the office opposite WorldWise's: its opaque doors bore the words ALTERNATIVE ENERGIES. He raised an inquisitive eyebrow.

'You working with that lot?'

'Yes. I mean, just for a few days. Doing an ad to raise money.'

'Fun and games in there, is it, since all that business happened?'

'It's a bit intense,' Tim agreed. 'Makes me wish I was working on solar panels.'

'You what, mate?'

'Oh.' Tim sighed inwardly at his ongoing struggle with small talk. 'Just, I assumed you worked for Alternative Energies.'

'Ah.' The man twinkled amused comprehension. 'I do, but it's not an energy company. It's your nips and your tucks.'

'Plastic surgery?'

'We call it cosmetic surgery more nowadays. What we do:

we do bespoke trips. People come over from the UK, they have a holiday, they get implants at the same time. Get the boobs done, or the lipo. And then, a lot of Dubai girls trying to get skin-lightening prescriptions and that. Which, being as it's a free zone, there are obviously restrictions, but we find ways round.'

Tim tried to pick what he could from this speech. 'Why ... so why are you called Alternative Energies?'

The surgery salesman spread his arms in cheerful help-lessness. 'Couldn't tell you, mate. Sounds good, I suppose.'

After the man had gone, Tim stood gazing out over the city: the knife-topped towers, the bored sun, and the encampments of construction yellow. Along the Sheikh Zayed Road, which he'd been driven along only days before, new people were being ushered in, new people every moment, chasing whatever it was they had heard was here.

As soon as Tim entered, Christian grabbed his arm like an over-keen holiday rep and steered him to the conference table where the rest of the team were already sitting. 'Right, that's everyone! We're ready to rock and roll!'

But there was little sense of rock and roll around the table. A humidity of spent words hung in the air. Jo was shaking her head slowly in apparent grievance; Ruth's mane of hair sloped wearily over her shoulders; Bradley stared down at the table. Miles's chicken-drumstick arms were folded defensively. Only Christian seemed his usual self. If anything, with his top button undone and his eyes blazing from a face framed with a little more stubble, he was more like himself than ever.

'Things have been tough, obviously,' said Christian. 'But I want you to remember what we're fighting for here. For people's lives.' There it was again, Tim thought: the statesmanlike energy, the showy gleam of his phrases. 'We're going to get this project back on track today. We've got this afternoon and tomorrow at the golf club and then we've still got more filming days if we need them. We can do this, guys.'

On the way down to the cars, Roper put his hand on Tim's arm again. 'Can I ask you about something?'

Tim thought of Jo with an inner lurch of panic. 'Of course.'

'Have you had a chance to think about tinkering with the script?'

'Ah.' Tim exhaled. 'Yes. I thought, instead of "send money straight to where it makes a difference", we could just say something like "you can join the fight against poverty".'

He'd made it up on the spot, and it sounded laughably vague, but Christian was nodding with satisfaction like a connoisseur rolling a wine around his palate. 'Join the fight. Join the fight. Yes. That's great, Tim. Really great.'

The WorldWise vehicle collected them, as ever, a few

paces from the entrance to the Centrepiece, and picked its way horizontally across five lanes of traffic. Hip-hop was playing on the radio; almost every other word was blanked out, so it sounded as if the recording artist had a severe case of hiccups. The driver glided into a new lane under a hail-storm of horns; nobody flinched. Tim looked at the shooting schedule. Everything with the project was still going ahead, as Christian had been so keen to stress.

At the golf club, security melted away with a couple of words from the Fixer, as usual, and the car slowed through a diagram of paths approaching a colonial-style building, French windows looking out over a veranda. On either side of the car, the greens and fairways spread out like a sea. From above, Tim thought, it would look even more like one: the light/dark variegations, the patches of surprising, inscrutable activity. Tim squinted quizzically at a floodlight pylon towering over a fairway.

'For night golf,' said the Fixer. 'It's too hot to play in the day. In the day, it's largely a golf club in name only.'

Sure enough the course was mostly deserted, though they passed a couple of men, one in a white shirt and one in pink, crouched over a golf ball as if examining the egg of a rarely seen species. The car let them out on the drive. A sponsor-funded piece of signage said PLAY THE GAME! Tim thought of the promotional video from the hotel, of the smoothly styled man swishing the ball in hot sun, the way this communicated – to some people – something like happiness.

Tim surveyed the building's wood-lined corridors, which revealed various uses beyond golf. There were numerous boardrooms, a 'relaxation room' and a games room. Next to the games room was a store cupboard, and as Tim approached, a staff member – with the diminutive stature and shuffling, keen-to-please demeanour he saw everywhere since Ashraf's departure – emerged from this cupboard, giving Tim a rather flustered smile.

When the man had gone, Tim glanced over his shoulder and peeked into the cupboard. Shelves heaved with groceries. Partly obscured by a bottle of olive oil was a laminated list headed *A GENTLE REMINDER!*

Smile at everyone.

If cleaning or hoovering, do this unobtrusively.

If clearing away food, ensure guest has finished with plate and is not offended by sudden withdrawal.

Do not ask about the winners of golf games, etc. Limit conversation to, e.g. 'I hope you are enjoying your time with us, sir.'

Always remember that people are here to relax and enjoy themselves, and you to work.

Tim was about to close the cupboard again when he caught sight of a door handle. Feeling like an ill-informed version of James Bond, he reached out, turned it, and found himself in what could only be called a hidden room.

It was a library, decorated like the salon of some English landowner, with shooting sticks and muskets in glass cabinets and portraits of whiskered men on the walls, some of them wielding golf clubs or accompanied by dogs of suitably grandiose bearing. Tim could not tell if any of them depicted a real man or whether they had been made in a generic aristo-portrait style. Sherry and port sat in crystal decanters. The drone of running machines came incongruously through the wall. Tim ran his eyes along the bookshelves, which were coated in literary armour: Dickens, Trollope, Galsworthy. A gaudy paperback by Joanna Trollope had been inserted between the Barchester novels.

On his way back to the lounge, Tim ran into Jo. It was the first time they had been alone together since that night on the balcony. He offered her a clumsy smile; her dark eyes went calmly over his face.

'Everything ready to go?' asked Tim as breezily as he could.

'Yes,' said Jo, 'it's going to be good. We're going to get right back on track.' It was almost an exact echo of what her husband had said earlier, and Tim had the unpalatable feeling he was being brushed off, managed by automatic replies. He cleared his throat.

'Look, about the other night.'

This had a more dramatic effect than he had banked on, or even wished for: Jo's eyebrows shot up in alarm, and her face lost its colour. It looked pallid now, even by the corridor's discreet lighting. 'What do you mean?'

'What happened between us . . .' Tim shifted weight nervously from one foot to the other. 'I'm really sorry if—'

'Oh!' Jo touched him on the arm. Tim felt his skin tingle. 'I thought . . . never mind.'

'You thought I meant something else?'

'I thought you meant the night Raf died.'

'No. Why? What happened that night?'

'Nothing. Nothing. I got confused.' Jo's grip was hard on his wrist now. Tim could feel his restraint and decency gearing up for another battle with desire; and this time from a weakened position, barely recovered from the last onslaught. 'Look, I'm sorry if I was too pushy,' Jo said, in a murmur.

'You weren't. I just lost my nerve.'

'Well, do you have your nerve this time?' asked Jo. She piloted him through the door marked Relaxation Room. Tim dimly registered a series of futons, separated by silk curtains. He thought she was going to take him to one of them, but they stopped dead in the middle of the room and Jo kissed him. He yielded to her; the kiss was followed by another and another. Tim was dizzy and appalled at himself, and also thrilled. Mostly thrilled, he thought; then, as footsteps sounded alarmingly nearby, mostly appalled.

'I'll go first,' said Jo, almost in a whisper, and he heard her greet someone – a staff member, a neutral voice. As he walked back into the lounge, Tim felt his legs might be about to give way. There were a handful of members here now, ageing Westerners with whiskies or pints of Guinness in front of them, English newspapers spread out on the tables; Tim skulked among them until Ruth announced that it was time to get out on the course.

Sprinklers sent water in shimmering arcs onto the greens. Miles was patrolling a gantry of scaffolding like a mad old king, fixing a camera to a mechanical arm, using a loudhailer to boom instructions to those below. Bradley removed his baseball cap.

'Speed. Camera. And . . . OK, go.'

'What if I told you an unbelievable fact? By 2016, 1 per cent of the world's population will own more than 99 per cent of its wealth. And that's while there are people starving. Like I said: unbelievable. But then, sometimes—'

'—And cut.'

'Sorry.' One of the camera assistants was shaking his head. 'Something on the lens. Sorry. Five minutes.'

'And parasol for Jason, please,' called Ruth, swatting hair out of her pink face.

From the paltry shelter of a clump of thin trees, used by the crew as a holding area for equipment, Tim watched with the continuity lady and the photographer as Jason Streng went about his work. Occasionally a couple of golfers would approach, speculate noisily as to Jason's identity, and em- bark on a circuitous conversation to recall where they had seen him before. Twice Tim took on the job of shushing or dismissing these people, but the second time he was too late: their chat caused the shot to be abandoned once more. Streng seemed more amused than impatient. He goofed around, playing shots with an imaginary golf club; he waved away the parasol-proffering youngster. 'I'm not a china doll, man. I won't break.' When Bradley called for him to walk again, he re-enacted exactly the steps he had taken, each flicker of the face, and each word of the spiel until he was cut off again.

After a couple of hours, they had got the establishing shot they wanted, and Miles was almost ready for the 'flying' scene. Still clogged with adrenalin from earlier events, and with a growing sense that the advert was – after all – getting 'back on track', Tim felt his spirits lift. The excitement at watching his idea come to life, which had been smothered by everything since he arrived, now began to spark again. It was still a tragedy, what had happened to Raf – of course it was – but work had to go on, life had to go on.

Elaine, Jason's agent, was wearing a pair of tan shades that swallowed her eyes entirely, giving her an appearance of alien hybridity. Christian and Jo were standing well apart, their body language suggesting different agendas, different mindsets – or was that just what Tim thought he saw, what he was happy to see? Christian joined Miles on the gantry as the cameraman began to holler through his loudhailer.

'OK. WE WILL BE GOOD TO GO IN FIVE, PLEASE. LISTEN TO BRADLEY AND LET'S GET THIS DONE. LET'S NOT WAVE OUR DICKS ABOUT, PLEASE.'

'Everyone to first positions,' ordered Bradley. 'I need – I need one of those things myself, here.'

As soon as he had said this, the Fixer appeared on the gantry steps. He swung nimbly down and handed a loud-hailer to the director. There was a horrible screech of feed-back as Bradley pressed the wrong button. For ten seconds there was a collective daze, as if gas had been sprayed into the air.

The hum of a golf buggy came from behind them. Elaine,

the agent, was waving the script at Bradley: 'I've just got a couple of things I need to query.' The thrum of the engine became louder; a buggy, driven by a man in a dishdash and keffiyeh, pulled up and out hopped Adam. There came a threatening cry from Christian Roper, up on the gantry. He seized the loudhailer from Miles.

'WHAT THE FUCK ARE YOU DOING HERE?'

Tim looked at Adam, his sleeves rolled up in that old-school hack way, his features in a whimsical smile, like someone confident of making a good impression at a party.

'DO YOU WANT TO COME UP HERE AND EXPLAIN WHY I SHOULDN'T HAVE YOU THROWN OFF THE PREMISES?' yelled Christian Roper, his voice robbed of its normal authority by the loudhailer, which gave him the appearance of an out-of-control traffic cop or a street evangelist.

'I'd be happy to,' said Adam, with a thumbs-up, and Tim watched as he approached the gantry at the same time as Elaine.

'WE HAVE A SCRIPT QUERY HERE,' Bradley shouted into his own loudhailer, 'SO I'M SENDING THE TALENT'S AGENT UP TO CHECK IN WITH YOU ABOUT IT.'

'WE DON'T HAVE ALL THE TIME IN THE WORLD,' Miles yelled back, the two of them bellowing as if one was on Earth and the other on the Moon. Elaine shook off her shoes and got onto the first step; Adam, carrying some sort of recording device, was close behind. Christian Roper was still shouting and gesturing, his words disappearing into the sky. Jo had moved towards the gantry now and obstructed Adam's path.

'Leave it,' said Jo. 'I would not go up there.'

'Your husband,' said Adam, with calm mockery, 'specifically invited me up there.'

'Leave it.' Jo's arm was on his shoulder.

'I NEED THIS AREA CLEAR!' appealed Miles.

They all looked up, but by the time they had registered the struggle on the gantry there was something else, something terrible. A cry split the air, coming from several people at once. Miles's voice was loudest in the mix. Someone – no, something – was falling towards them. 'Look out!' a voice shouted, and they scattered, but it had already landed. A camera lay mangled, glass fragments glimmering, the metal frame like a mass of dislocated bones.

'Jesus Christ,' said Ruth faintly, getting down onto her haunches as if to inspect the damage; but she stayed where she was, her head on her knees. Jo Roper lowered herself to the ground and put a hand on Ruth's shoulder. Tim joined them, as much as anything because he felt as if he might faint. He reached out for Ruth's other shoulder, feeling the tautness of her breaths as she tried to stop herself from shaking. Adam swallowed and licked his lips and then, recovering himself, rapidly took three photographs.

They stayed there, the three of them, any one of whom would surely have been killed if the fallen camera had hit them. Tim could feel Ruth's shoulders rising and falling. Above them, from the gantry, no sound came at all. Tim could hear a trickling noise which in the moment he almost took for the sound of someone bleeding, but it was just a sprinkler, somewhere out across the fairway, continuing its endless maintenance of the lawn.

Even the Fixer seemed somehow defeated by this latest set-back: instead of the two cars he had ordered, a solitary one turned up, and it was obviously too small to take them all back. Miles, who had changed T-shirts and was carrying the discarded one like a dishcloth, loaded the remaining equipment into the boot.

'I've been working with these cameras for twenty-five years,' he said, to himself or to the group, it was not quite clear. 'I could set up one of these in my sleep. And I tell you what, that camera did not just fall. Someone pushed it. That camera,' he repeated, 'did not just fall.'

The members of the group avoided eye contact. Tim tried to remember exactly what had happened, to visualize the seconds leading up to it, to recall who had been where. Perhaps there was someone a few feet away from him who knew what had happened; who knew what had happened to Raf, too, for that matter. He had the sensation of a mesh moving closer to all of them, ready to contract around him.

'There's no way we're going to be shooting again tomorrow,' Miles continued with gloomy relish. 'That camera is shafted. It's fucked beyond repair. And we're not going to be able to replace it without at least a couple of days' notice. Yeah, make no mistake: that thing is shot to shit.' He went on in this vein, making his point in yet more emphatic terms, although nobody was contradicting him. The rest of the team shuffled around the issue of car-space and Tim saw a chance to be useful – if only by absenting himself.

'I don't mind staying here, getting them to call me a cab.'

'If you're sure,' replied the Fixer instantly, as though he had made Tim say this with a conjuring trick. 'That would be good. I can send one for you within the half-hour. You could have a drink here.' He mustered a semblance of one of his grins. 'Talk golf with some of the guys.'

As he watched the car pull away – Ruth staring blankly out of the window, the Fixer already on the phone – Tim's momentary alarm at being left alone quickly gave way to relief; he felt the net, the invisible trap, shrink away just a little. He had no appetite for the new round of loaded conversations, of glances and insinuations, that would come now; and he was best off away from Jo, and from anyone who might suspect them. He would be better off, perhaps, away from here altogether. Maybe I could go home, he told himself. I should go home to London. They don't actually need me here, and it doesn't feel safe.

'What are you doing out here, man? Soaking up the rays?'

It was Jason Streng, his agent following at a vigilant distance. He lowered his sunglasses and cocked his head at Tim.

'Oh. Er. They couldn't fit me in the car, so . . .'

'You can ride with us, man,' said Jason, in his strange cod-American accent. Or maybe it was the word 'ride' that seemed odd: as if they were planning a beachside cruise rather than leaving the scene of a near-fatality. As he slid into the back seat of an SUV not much smaller than a mini-bus, Tim was conscious of a quick exchange of looks and shrugs between Streng and Elaine, and suspected that she was questioning the wisdom of this move. To hell with her, thought Tim with a sort of tired defiance. I've got a right to be here. What does she think I'm going to do to him?

'Just shove those out of the way if you want,' said Streng from the front seat, indicating a collection of white laminated shopping bags decorated with single words like SOUL and SANCTUARY; words that in another context, Tim thought, would mean important things. There was no need to move them, though: the vehicle was bigger than the ones used to ferry the entire team about, and Tim was able to sit a comfortable distance from Elaine, whose nails tap-danced across the buttons of her phone as they carved through the traffic.

They passed the Dubai Pearl billboard, THE FUTURE IS TODAY, and Tim – wanting to say something innocuous and witty – muttered: 'That's funny, I thought the future was further off than that.'

'Sorry, what?' said Jason. Elaine glanced momentarily at Tim as if, even by speaking this much, he was in some way imperilling her client.

'Oh, just that billboard. For the new housing development. Seems a bit – a bit of a silly slogan.'

Jason said nothing at all; it seemed, incredibly, that Tim had somehow managed to offend him, or maybe he was just too bored by the feebleness of the conversation even to enter into it. But just as Tim felt an outsider's sorrow wrap itself around his shoulders once more, Streng swung around to look at him.

'A mate of mine, Noel Shaw.' He said the name as if Tim would inevitably know it; Tim nodded obligingly. 'Great guy. Comes out here a few years ago, goes to one of these property sales. A sales guy tells him about the Palm. The dude says if he takes a villa there and then, he can get two more villas for half price.'

Streng was enthused by his own tale, Tim was pleased to see: performance, after all, was what he did. He slipped between the voices of the two characters in his anecdote – Noel a sleazy-sounding American, the salesman breathy and wheedling – and Tim began to relax. 'So of course Noel says, why the fuck would I want to buy *three* villas! The sales guy says: you can flip them.'

'Flip them?'

'Flip them. There's a line outside to buy these properties. You come out of here and say you've got three, you can double your money. Straight away. And you know what he did?'

'He bought them?'

'He bought them.' Streng laughed, and Tim laughed with him. 'He drops, like, a million bucks there and then. He goes outside. It's just like the guy said. He sells two of the villas, literally right there. And you know what the buyers will have done?'

'Sold them on again?'

'Exactly. Flipped them straight on. Probably to people in the same line, ten minutes later. And so on. And I tell you the really fucking mad thing. None of these places existed yet. This was all off-plan. So they get bought and sold, bought and sold ten times before a brick's been laid.'

'And what exactly do you do, Tim?' asked Elaine, cutting in, in a cold voice which stalled Tim's confidence surge. He swallowed.

'I, I'm a creative.'

'But what does that actually mean?'

'I've done a few campaigns for Vortex. Coming up with ideas; selling them to the client.'

'Anything I would have heard of?'

Even before the prize-nominated Yorkshire campaign, Tim had had some notable successes. There was 'SOME-TIMES YOU'VE GOT NO CHOICE' for a chocolate company – a series of ads in which people desperate for the product were shown lying in wait with baseball bats, ripping snack bars away from children. There'd been a handful of complaints, enough for the campaign to go down as a winner. Then there was a series of print ads for a hotel group involving a long-faced, post-coital couple: the slogan said 'WELL, OUR BEDS AREN'T THE PROBLEM'. After the ad the models had allegedly embarked on a real-life affair. It was only a story, but it got into a trade journal, so it was better than if it had been true.

He started trying to describe the latter campaign to Elaine, whose face not only betrayed a lack of recognition, but barely changed at all. By the time they got out of the car, what mileage Tim had felt he'd gained was lost again. He said goodbye to Streng and his agent with the odd feeling that it was possible he wouldn't see them again. Tomorrow there would be, quite likely, no more filming; and beyond tomorrow, he was beginning to feel, he would have left Dubai.

Late afternoon was giving way to evening, but the heat had only dropped a little; reggae and samba music floated from pools where bathers still lay, slumped like toy animals, and children called shrilly and splashed one another.

Unsure whether to eat at one of the beachside places or go back to Maritime Tower, Tim scanned a couple of menus, unable to summon any real appetite even when managers emerged and boasted of various 'very special' dinner deals, which sounded a lot like the ones they'd advertised every other time he had passed. A couple of places were already doing a good trade: waiters moved busily like ants. He sat eventually on a terrace and tried to collect his thoughts.

He wondered how he could have fielded Elaine's blunt enquiry – what exactly do you do? – in a manner that would have sounded more convincing. Clearly, he'd done well for somebody not even out of his twenties. It was just that everything here was so far from the parameters within which he normally measured his life. In this warren of eating-places, amid these palaces of luxury goods and tab-leaux of pure leisure upon which even a death made no more than a momentary scratch, he was unmoored from the sort of reality that made his achievements seem real. Mentioning his award nomination here, or indeed his whole showreel, would mean about as much as getting out his school swimming certificates.

A waitress was standing a little way away, studiously not looking at him, arms folded, an internationally recognized waiting-for-an-order stance. Tim asked for a Coke. His brain registered the taste before it was in his mouth; Coke was so familiar that there was hardly any difference between drinking it and not drinking it. Perhaps that was part of the problem with the Village, he thought: everything was so well managed, so perfect, that nothing really mattered at all.

As Tim finished the drink and joined the central path marked out by the mock-weathered signposts, this unreal feeling began to take hold of him more firmly. The tear-shaped swimming pool, childishly blue; the magazines and airport thrillers, the waiters and lifeguards. None of this is really happening, he thought, with a sensation like dizziness or sickness. Inside the lift in Maritime Tower he took a deep breath, exhaling as the doors shut. He pressed the button and then ran his hands slowly over the lift wall, and the moment of intense dissociation seemed to pass. It's fine, he said to himself. You are in Dubai. Things are a little strange, that's all.

He decided to focus purely on the normal, the minute-by-minute; not on Raf's death and the mysteries and uncertainties multiplying by the hour. He'd allowed his brain to overfill.

Outside, it was beginning to get dark, and the sight was comforting. For a few moments, as the orange sun plunged into the sea, Tim felt a certain awe for Dubai again, even an affection, as if it were a still-attractive person about whom he'd discovered something disappointing. The Burj Al Arab gazed across the water at him, the panels of its body lit in seductive gradations of blue, and Tim had the fleeting fantasy that someone in the higher reaches of the tower was looking out towards him, like they were two turret prisoners in a fairytale.

As usual, the dark that succeeded the dusk fixed a fluttering alarm somewhere in Tim's stomach. He ran a bath and ordered room service, which was brought by a sadly smiling Filipino. Then he switched on his laptop, glancing at the screensaver's two-dimensional Burj.

There was an email from Stan to the whole company about new business, a campaign for a male perfume called Utopia 'created' by a pop star who was barely aware of its existence. There was nothing from Rod, as Tim had hoped there might be, to explain the curtailment of their call. And once the inbox was exhausted, there was the inevitability of his next Google search. Reading about anything other than Raf's death felt like being one of the people who, minutes after it was announced, went back to smiling and tending the swimming pools. Within an hour of vowing to disengage from the theme, Tim was reading a blog by one of Raf's friends.

The friend took up the theme that there was a conspiracy. Dubai, claimed the writer, was a Wild West in which money could solve any problem, 'including the problem of someone being alive whom you want to be dead'. Tim clicked a link to another blog and felt his hands freeze on the keyboard.

> I've got a certain amount of interest in this case, not just because I spent three years working in Dubai – as regular readers will know – but because, believe it or not, I vaguely know one of the people involved in the case, the guy from the Vortex agency.

Tim read these lines several times before scrolling down to the bottom of the page to discover the identity of the writer. His name was Marcus Carless. A memory-bell rang in a vault of his brain. It was a boy from his class at school. It was a stretch to say they 'vaguely' knew each other, after all this time. Tim couldn't even picture his face: his memories were all of the name itself, with its peculiar half-rhyme. Carless was now apparently some sort of financial analyst, one of the many people who'd popped into Dubai for the gold rush.

However many times Tim read the sentence, he could not make the words mean what they claimed to mean: that he, Tim, was one of a handful of people who could legitimately be accused of committing a murder. Of course, there was absolutely no evidence there had even been a murder, but Carless seemed in little doubt. The 'drink and drugs cocktail' found in Raf's bloodstream was nothing more than a convenient phrase, he wrote, absolving all but the victim. Everyone knew that illicit behaviour went on in Dubai, and the authorities turning a blind eye was part of the deal by which the whole city maintained its survival. But this was still the United Arab Emirates, and now and again they liked a salutary example. Westerners have sex on the beach: they get thrown into prison. A guy takes the partying too far: he dies in his hotel suite. The moral: Dubai can be tough if it has to be. More and more Westerners arrive on the promise of sex and parties; they stay just on the right side of the law; everyone is happy. But there'd be another autopsy, Carless predicted: that was the least Raf and his family deserved.

Besides, added the writer casually, it was hardly as if WorldWise was completely above board; how's Dubai Pearl going? he asked, rhetorically, adding a whimsical sort of winking smile constructed from a bracket and a semi-colon.

Even accounting for the fact that this man had lived in Dubai, it was dizzying and unpleasant how blasé he was about the supposed facts of the situation; the breezy way he predicted a 'second autopsy', when Tim could not even find reference, on the internet, to the results of the first one. And Carless was only one of a gathering mass of people mystery-solving from a distance in this recreational way, while Tim and his colleagues flailed about, fielding the suggestive looks of strangers. They, the people closest to the situation, were the only ones unable to see it: it was as if they were pieces in a jigsaw puzzle.

Tim slammed the lid of the laptop shut and pushed it away.

He remembered the Facebook post he'd read before, the ominous cliché: 'Some1 knows something'. The internet was rapidly making him feel that too many people knew too many things. So many opinions were laid out as facts. Each pieced-together version of the last moments of Raf Kavanagh's life was real to the person who thought it. Tim had the weird and not entirely articulated feeling that there might not *be* a real story: that the reality of what had happened to Raf might sink beneath the weight of all the versions which were not true, yet still existed.

There were footsteps outside, approaching along the corridor. The footsteps stopped and there was a startling knock at the door.

'Hello?' Tim called.

But nobody spoke. The air-conditioning's hum went on, neutral as ever, one unending breath. Tim called out again; once more there was no reply. Then, two more knocks. For a second he experienced fear of a strain purer than any he had ever known. It began in his crotch, like an erection would, but it was the opposite of that feeling – a creeping cold, spreading upwards and downwards simultaneously. He imagined himself opening the door and looking into the eyes of someone who had committed murder, knowing that he was next. Don't be an idiot, he thought. Nobody can get in. Also, there's a peephole on the door. You can just go and look through the peephole.

But he stayed where he was; it felt as if some greater force than himself was pinning him down. His thoughts went back to what he'd read, to the remark about Raf 'deserving' a second autopsy. He pictured Raf's family waiting at the airport: some windswept stretch of tarmac, staff in hi-vis jackets standing indifferently by.

After fifteen or twenty minutes which seemed considerably longer, Tim at last felt the tension begin to recede. If someone was listening, they would have realized there was nothing much to hear. Tim allowed himself to get up and go about what business he could find. He put on the spotlights at either side of the bed; he switched on the TV and listened with relief to the foreign-language jabber of a football commentator.

He peeled his shorts off and set the shower to London Rain, which proved a successful adaptation of the real thing: it was cold, low-to-medium intense, steady and plodding. He felt the cleansing touch of it on his back and shoulders. There'd never been anyone at the door, he told himself. Or if there had, it was room service, housekeeping; one of the army of staff who had worked out they were not wanted. The water rushed over him. Soon, very soon, he could be back in London.

When he came out of the shower, a *Poirot* was on TV: the coincidence brought the ghost of a smile to Tim's lips. He opened the laptop and the screen sprang obediently to life once more. There had been too many hints about World-Wise; it was clear he should have been more diligent in researching the charity before he came here. Did Raf find out something they didn't want him to know? There was little chance of discovering anything on the internet other than another mountain of conjecture, but he would look it up, even so. On the screen, Poirot – brow furiously furrowed beneath that eggshell cranium – lamented that he had been an idiot, twenty-three times an idiot; his wingman Hastings gaped in trademark incomprehension.

When Tim turned his eyes back to the laptop, he was confronted with a row of black text in Arabic, topped by an exclamation mark. He tried again to get onto it; once more he received the message, polite but non-negotiable, like the red light rejecting his room card. He tried Facebook, then the BBC site: the same thing happened.

He called down to the Centrepiece and was asked if he minded going on hold, then was instantly placed on hold anyway. A recorded voice reminded him that the Village had a range of world-class leisure facilities. Tim reached into the minibar and opened a bottle of white wine.

From the moment you step into the Village, the voice was saying, you will feel at home. It's a place where business can be a pleasure, and where pleasure is our business. With executive accommodation across a range of luxurious blocks . . .

Tim looked back at the screen. Why was he blocked from the web, and why was the message not in English, in this resort so tailored to foreign custom that its native language had virtually been obliterated? He stared in frustration at the dance of symbols across the screen, symbols which a different person could convert into words and ideas.

Go online to find out more, he was now being entreated by the recorded message – a suggestion which seemed ironic in the current circumstances – and to discover our partner companies, which include Dubai Pearl, where the future . . .

Where the future is now, thought Tim with a tiresome sense of déjà vu. Then something happened in his brain, or several things all at once. He remembered reading those words on the hoarding, commenting sarcastically; Jason's complete blankness. He thought of the momentary panic in Elaine's eyes every time somebody approached Jason, her insistence on filtering all requests; about the secret they were nursing together, referred to in the trailer. He sloshed a glass of wine out of the bottle. What if Jason had been non-plussed by the billboard because he didn't know what it said, just as Tim couldn't make out the words on his laptop screen? What if Jason could not read?

The more he thought about it, the more plausible it was. It would explain why Jason had to be chaperoned everywhere, why nobody was allowed to speak to him directly; why scripts had to be delivered via his agent. What had seemed the power of his position – declining to sign things, sidestepping tedious admin – might really be about the precariousness of it. If it came out that he couldn't read, well, it might not be the end of his career, but it would certainly be embarrassing and debilitating. If Tim was right, it would be a secret worth defending by almost any means; that is, if anyone knew it. Someone like Raf. But this was all amateur-sleuth stuff again, thought Tim as he slid back against the propped-up pillows on the bed: he might as well be in the *Poirot*, where the characters were being asked to assemble in the library for the detective's verdict. Tim was filled with the wish to be back in Devon, Mrs Callaghan chipping in with her own findings: 'Would you really *murder* someone for that, though, Henry?' His father replying gently: 'I personally wouldn't, no, love.'

What was big enough to justify a murder? Could Raf really have become a target because of this secret, if he had discovered it – if indeed there was anything to discover? The trouble was that 'motive' felt too indistinct an idea: as Bradley had implied, most people who committed a crime probably didn't wake up that day knowing that they were going to do it.

Shortly, Poirot would deliver answers. 'It was you who did it,' he would say, and one of the suspects' faces would twist in knee-jerk denial, and then finally flatten out in defeat. Like all the hard-bitten sleuths of other TV shows, the doddery-but-clever ones, the tortured-by-a-dark-past ones, the detective would have put together a series of logical but nearly impossible mental wriggles and joined the dots to the answer. That was what the viewer wanted: for death to be shocking, but ultimately explicable. No bank holiday special ended with its characters in Tim's predicament: unsure what had happened, let alone who was responsible. He hung up the phone, letting the recorded message – as he imagined – go on talking silently to itself.

Before preparing tomorrow's clothes and putting the light out, he finally unlocked the door, opening it an eighth of the way, then a quarter, and finally the full swing. Naturally, there was no one there. Looking left and right down the corridor he saw nothing but the purpose-built living space, which meant him no harm, which had been designed for people like him to switch off in, to forget their problems, to have all their desires fulfilled.

10: NOCTURNE

By lantern-light, Tim was walking towards Raf's chalet. He carried on. The door of the chalet was wide open. Raf greeted him with a regretful smile. 'I know what's coming,' he said. Tim's grip was tight on Raf's throat, and the next time he glanced down the face was lifeless and uncomprehending. Tim had sleepwalked to the chalet, found it open, murdered Raf Kavanagh and gone back to his own bed without being aware of it. He had done it because he hated Raf, nothing more than that; because he hated him, and was drunk enough to lose control of himself. He was a murderer, and everything else he'd done – the aggregation of everything he had strived for, and worked towards – meant nothing.

Then it was over and he wasn't screaming any more. His back was so plastered in sweat that it felt as if he were wearing some clinging garment. His face was feverish. He was in the corridor, with his back to the door of his room. Studded ceiling-lights shone on, like cat's eyes on a road, and it was neither night nor day.

Understanding came in unsteady spurts: he had sleep-walked out of his room. It was a dream, not a memory. Of course I didn't kill him, he thought, putting his hand to his heart, which was pumping ostentatiously in his bare chest. It was not possible to kill someone in your sleep, was it? With every second that followed, the dream seemed more flagrantly removed from reality. Tim marvelled at the idea something could be so real, and then so impossible.

It was only as he pushed the door that his current circumstances lined up properly in front of him. He was wearing only underpants, he was locked out of his room, and did not have a card to let himself back in.

Tim snorted at the stupidity of it and gave the door a couple of shoves in some spirit of feeble defiance. He sank down almost to his haunches, feeling the exhaustion of the nightmare in his limbs, and then got straight back up, thinking it was better to deal with this now. He would call down to somebody. But how? His hands went in an absurd phone-finding dance across his bare torso.

He could knock on someone's door and get them to phone down. Yes: that was obviously the answer. It was so simple to find a solution, if you took time and didn't panic. The trouble was that it was the middle of the night. He couldn't tell how long he'd slept before the bad dream had taken hold.

He went along the corridor to 733 and 734. Nobody responded to his cautious knocks. But at 735, the door was opened almost immediately, as if someone had been waiting for this. Tim jumped. At the sight of him, so did Adam, the journalist, whose large bottom lip curled upwards into a smile.

'Bit forward of you, but I'm flattered!'

Tim laughed sportingly. 'I've somehow locked myself out. In my . . . in my sleep.'

'Wow. Takes some doing.'

As he followed Adam into the room, Tim wondered whether there was some sceptical undertone to this remark. The room was laid out and lit with an elegance that made Tim feel abashed by his own lack of it. The two bedside lamps had been turned to face the wall, where they cast agreeable dish-sized pools of light. On Adam's laptop, four opened windows were arranged in a diamond against a desktop backdrop of the Manhattan skyline, rendered in such acute definition that Tim felt he could reach out and touch the cold fibreglass of the towers. There was the aroma of freshly brewed coffee in the air.

In the time it had taken Tim to notice all this, Adam had dialled somebody somewhere in the Village, and was now passing Tim the handset. With his other hand he indicated a towelling robe hanging in the wardrobe. Adam got back into the swivel armchair and gave the appearance of working, but Tim, labouring to put on the robe while holding the receiver to his ear, still felt under observation.

'Sir?'

'Hello. I'm Tim Callaghan in Room 732.' He was disagreeably conscious of his own voice, its attempt to sound dignified.

'Room 732 in which building, sir?'

How many buildings could there be in the complex with as many rooms as this? 'The Maritime Tower.'

Tim explained his predicament.

'And can you help me with your activation code, sir?'

'What?'

The voice at the end was good-humoured. 'You should have an activation code on your key card, sir. If you quote this, I am able to activate a range of room services which—'

'But I don't have the key card. I'm locked out.'

'If you try your key card on the sensor outside the door, sir—'

'I don't *have* the card. If I had the card I wouldn't be calling.'

Eventually Tim persuaded the man to get somebody to come up with a duplicate card. Adam swivelled his chair in

Tim's direction – though he was careful, Tim noticed, to shield the laptop screen – and gritted his teeth in comic frustration.

'They drive you mad, don't they!'

'He kept asking for a key card. But obviously, if I had the card . . .'

'If you had the card,' said Adam, rolling his eyes with such cartoonish eagerness that his eyebrows threatened to disappear over the top of his head, 'you would qualify for help, but you wouldn't need it. I mean, this whole place is catch-22, isn't it?'

'I haven't read *Catch-22*,' Tim admitted.

'Nor have I,' said Adam. He pointed to the coffee machine. Tim hesitated.

'I might struggle to get back to sleep. Not a worry for you, obviously.'

'No, I work when I work.' Adam shrugged. 'I work when there are stories to be written up.'

'When are there ever *not* stories?'

'Never.'

Tim looked at the journalist. They were roughly the same age; it was just the bags under the eyes, the rolled-up sleeves, that made Adam seem his senior. 'So you're always working?'

'I try to be.' Adam grinned. 'Work is more fun than fun, as

someone said. As a gay man, what else am I going to do around here? Go clubbing? Tea, then, if coffee doesn't float your boat?'

Tim found himself accepting this time, even though a triple knock on the door signalled the arrival of the sadly smiling Filipino girl from earlier, with a replacement card which she handed to Tim with a look of particular melancholy as if it were an item of some personal value to her. Now that he had the means of getting back into his room, it was all the clearer to Tim that he wasn't anxious to go there. He watched Adam open a silver tin of teabags; yes, Tim thought, he was just the sort of man to bring his own tea to a hotel.

'And what's the story here?' asked Tim, in a tone as light as he could make it.

'You tell me,' said Adam, his tone changing, becoming clipped and precise. 'Or maybe you tell me and I'll tell you. I've got some of it. You must have some of it.'

The kettle began a polite purr. Adam sat down in the armchair. Tim felt disconcerted by his honesty. It occurred to him that perhaps, in spite of his mannerisms and affectations, Adam might be the only person here certain to tell him the truth.

He handed Tim the tea. Its smell, suggestive of meeting-rooms in London, struck Tim as somehow reassuring.

'Is it true you can't be . . . openly gay here?' asked Tim. 'I mean, there must be places . . .?'

He'd only meant this as a conversational offering, picking up a lead. But Adam's body changed as if the response led him even closer to an anticipated checkmate.

'There are places,' said Adam, 'like there are places for anything in Dubai. There's nothing you can't *actually* do. Just things you can't be seen to do.' He scratched his nose, not taking his eyes off Tim. 'Do you know who was outside Raf's chalet?'

'When?'

Adam looked at him. 'Ashraf was sacked for telling reporters what he saw. He saw two people kissing outside the chalet, just before Raf was murdered. Do you know who they were?'

'How do you know this?' Tim countered.

'I tracked Ashraf down. After you mentioned he'd been laid off. I found him in Deira.'

'Is he all right?'

'Friend of yours?' Adam half smiled. Tim shifted unhappily in his chair.

'Well, no, but I . . . I liked him.'

'I gave him some money to talk to me. He asked me if I had more money for his brother. His brother's sleeping in the same dorm. There were ten of them there. Not very pleasant. I gave them what I had, but . . .'

Tim tried to dismiss his mental picture of the little man leaving in his ill-fitting jacket, and the idea of the brother. 'But he wouldn't tell you who the . . . who the people kissing were?'

'He said he didn't know.' This time Adam's pout contained some real chagrin. 'But someone knows.'

'Not me,' said Tim.

There was glamour to all this, this cut and thrust of journalists and detectives, clue-foraging, the piecing together of a case: it would be a great story to tell, eventually. It was just that he felt enervated by the whole business; he was almost too tired even to get out of the chair.

'Well, let me know if you suddenly remember anything.' Adam gave one of his knowing eyebrow-swoops. 'That's what they say in the movies, isn't it?'

The continued sardonic tone made Tim want to counterattack. 'Is it true you broke into Bradley's room?'

Adam's slow smile credited Tim with a little more insight than he'd previously allowed. 'Why do you ask?'

'He said you'd been poking around in there.'

'He's half right. I didn't do it. I draw the line at violations of privacy. I mean, beyond what's inevitable. But a colleague of mine feels less strongly about that principle.'

'How the fuck did he get into Bradley's room?'

Adam blinked in what might have been genuine surprise at the question. 'Just went down and claimed to be Bradley. The people here haven't got a clue who's who. You must have noticed that.' Adam sipped his coffee. 'Anyway. Aren't you going to ask what he found?'

Tim's guts swilled unpleasantly. *Was* he going to ask? He was far from sure that he wanted to know anything compromising about Bradley, or indeed about anyone.

'The place was covered – *covered* – in pieces of paper. The walls. Every surface. All of them about the ad. "What is the 'world of the commercial'?" "What is the 'message'?" Pages and pages of notes. Spider-graphs. Brainstorms. Word association, where he'd written the word CHARITY and then listed literally a hundred words that he thought of. Pencil-sketches of Jason Streng. I mean, the whole works. Like it was a movie.' Adam shook his head. 'The poor bugger. He deserves better than to work for Christian Roper.'

Though used to Adam's dismissiveness by now, to his ironic, undermining way, Tim baulked at this last sentence. He himself was working for Christian; they had all come here to do so because the cause was a noble one. If he allowed these ideas to be whipped away from him, all the effort and strain of the past few days, of the weeks that had gone into this, would come to seem meaningless. It was very important to hang on to the good in this experience.

'That's harsh,' said Tim. 'Whatever is going on with WorldWise – and I appreciate you know more than me – they've achieved a lot in the past.'

'In the past, yes,' said Adam. 'But I'm interested in the present. And in the present, people die on their watch, cameras topple down and nearly kill journalists.'

'You think it was aimed at you?'

'I didn't actually say that,' said Adam. 'The camera was, pretty obviously, pushed by whoever is covering up the facts of Raf's death, or whoever actually caused it. It could have been meant to hit any of the people standing there.' Tim's fatigued mind tried to follow Adam's along the route which made these huge statements so 'obvious' to him; he felt like one of the amateur skiers at the mall, slipping and sliding behind an instructor. 'I mean, you heard Miles: he was fairly emphatic on the subject of whether it could have fallen off that gantry.'

'But hang on, you weren't even there when he was talking about that.'

'The point,' said Adam, sailing past this reasonable objection, 'is that this is a dangerous place now. I have to stay here: it's my job. But if I were you, I'd be out of here very fast. I really would. I'd be out of here on the next plane.'

This was uttered with an apparent sincerity that Tim found somewhat startling, given Adam's track record of sniping; it made him wonder what facts Adam had in his possession that had not emerged in this conversation. He was the sort of person, Tim thought, to make you feel that he had not even delved into his top ten conversational gambits, was saving them for someone better. The fact that this was a posture – and an exasperating one – didn't necessarily mean it wasn't the case.

'I'm going to try and leave tomorrow,' Tim said, rising to his feet. The towelling robe swished around his frame and he realized he was going to have to walk out of the door with it; then he'd need to decide whether it was more embarrassing to return it, or not to.

'I think that's wise, I really do.' Again, this was offered almost as a plea, and the beseeching note seemed to surprise even Adam; they avoided eye contact for a moment by unspoken agreement. As Tim's hand found the door handle, though, Adam's tone changed again.

'You'll have to persuade Jo to let you go, though . . .'

Tim pivoted around. Adam's face wore its professional impertinence. His eyes bulged with mock contrition. 'Sorry. Gauche of me.'

'How do you know about . . .'

Adam winked. 'I think everyone knows.'

Tim's stomach flipped. There was no response to this; he felt outflanked and claustrophobic. He turned the door handle, half expecting Christian to be right outside, waiting to confront him. Had it been Christian knocking earlier? Had the camera been aimed at *him*?

The last thing Tim noticed as he left was an overnight bag slumped in a corner. An airline baggage tag bore the same date he himself had flown out here. Adam, then, had not come out after Raf's death. He'd been here all along.

What did this mean? It was one more thing to think about, and he had too many questions as it was. The new card let him back into his room, where the half-discarded sheet hung off the bed like wreckage. The radio was playing a delicate classical tinkle. It must be some alarm setting, Tim told himself, some automatic thing, like the air-con, like every other system here that existed more or less independently of the residents. 'Chopin's famous Nocturne in E Minor—' began a college-polished voice, as Tim jabbed at the panel and shut off the sound.

Yes, there were too many things to think about, but three connected ideas were uppermost in Tim's brain as he pulled the sheet back across the mattress. First, he should not have become involved with Jo. Secondly, he might be in danger even regardless of that, because after what had happened with the camera it felt as if everyone was. Thirdly, he had to get out of Dubai, and off this account, and perhaps think about doing something else with his life, something that wouldn't bring him into contact with another situation like this. But to do that, he was going to have to leave this building in the morning, and for now it was difficult to imagine even stepping out of the door.

Although he hadn't known the piece of music, Tim felt as if he could still hear it in his head, and when he dispelled it, it was replaced by the tapping of Adam's fingers on the keyboard as – a couple of rooms down – he maintained his night watch over the story. When Tim shut his eyes, the image of Raf's face swam powerfully into view once more. He screwed his eyes tighter and put his hands over his face, until all the pictures were replaced by a fuzz like television interference, the white noise that had been crackling since time began.

11: THE GAME

He had fallen asleep with some idea that the mere act of pro-
gressing from one day to another would release him from his
problems, but it only took a look at his phone to destroy that
notion. A text from Christian informed him that they would
be meeting at noon, to go back to the golf club, 'as originally
scheduled'.

Tim's stomach was tightly knotted, and he felt a groggi-
ness that recalled the hangover on the morning they had all
found out: one of the last feelings he had registered when he
was still ignorant of the tragedy. He sank onto the toilet and
tried to order his thoughts. 'As originally scheduled.' The
attempted nonchalance of the text was at best rather disin-
genuous, he thought, and at worst almost psychopathically
indifferent: it was hardly part of the 'schedule' that a camera
had toppled and come within inches of smashing someone's
skull, was it?

Or, he reflected grimly as he adjusted the shower to

Normal setting, perhaps it *had* been on someone's itinerary. In any case, this was not a place he wanted to be any more. Foggy as his memory of the early-hours conversation with Adam was, he remembered with clarity the warning that it might be best to leave. It would not represent any sort of a climbdown, Tim told himself. There'd been a suspicious death, possibly a murder; yesterday, another near-fatality. There was every indication, despite Christian's text, that the ad would not get finished any time soon. And even if it did, Tim's role amounted to little more than changing a word here and there. There had never really been any point in his being here, you could argue; the role of 'creative' might just about mean something in an office, but here it was just a word, like everything was. He called Vortex in London and was put through to Stan.

'How's it going, mate? I would have been in touch sooner, but Louise, seriously. The woman is the bane of my life. Can you honestly tell me – right, you're a man of the world. What would you consider a "reasonable time" for someone to get up and feed a baby when they've been out all night at a—'

'Look, Stan,' said Tim. 'Sorry to interrupt. I need to get home. I don't think I should stay here any more.'

He tried to describe what had happened at the golf club. It was not easy to recount the events into the void of the phone line: there weren't even any encouraging hums or clicks of the tongue, since Stan had developed the skill of maintaining complete silence during a call, as a technique to extract concessions from whoever he was negotiating with. Even the pay-off – the brush with death – sounded oddly undramatic as Tim brought it to a close.

'I mean, seriously,' he said, in an attempt at a suitably grave epilogue, 'I could have been killed there and then.'

'That's terrible, mate,' said Stan, but it was not enough; it was the same sort of 'terrible' as Mum's book-club gossipers would apply to Raf's death, hinting at satisfaction, even excitement, that something so dramatic could happen so close at hand, yet harmlessly to oneself.

'So I need to get out,' Tim pressed. 'I was wondering if Vortex could sort a flight out. Change my ticket.'

'But you don't think someone is trying to get *you*?'

'No,' Tim conceded, 'not exactly, but . . .'

As soon as this backtrack was made, Tim felt as if he had weakened his position; as if it would now be too difficult to explain why his situation felt as wretched as it did.

'But I really do think I should get out of here,' he tried again.

'I think . . .' said Stan, his voice displaying not so much reluctance as a certain calm that was at odds with the reality confronting Tim. 'I think you'd need to talk to WorldWise, mate. I mean, they're the ones who booked the tickets. They're probably your best bet.'

This would all be perfectly sensible from Stan's point of view, because he wasn't here; all he knew of WorldWise was the sheen of their website, the stack of emails they'd sent finalizing the deal. Besides, Stan had his own problems, as did everyone; nobody could care about everything. Nobody *had* to care about anybody else's life, technically. That was why Tim had liked the idea of the WorldWise account in the first place. The idea was that it was an easy way of caring, or at least simulating care with a donation. It had all sounded so good, even a few days ago.

'The thing is,' Tim tried to explain, 'I'm not sure WorldWise are going to be much use with this. They're not in the best shape. I mean, the guy who originally arranged my flights is dead, to put things in context.'

'I can call them for you,' said Stan. 'Put in a word.'

'It's OK,' said Tim, 'I'm sure I . . . I'm sure it will be fine.'

'Look, I'll put you on to someone in HR,' said Stan, and before Tim could object he was listening to the hold-message that had been concocted in front of his own eyes, in the Shoreditch office. The words 'Vortex: a place where normal laws do not apply' were intoned, in a sort of mock-Hollywood twang, over some ironically resurgent Eighties pop song. Even the normal laws of hold music do not apply here, the sequence implied, in that oh-so-clever way Tim feared was typical of everything the agency did. He put the phone down.

I need to go home, Tim heard himself think on a loop, as the WorldWise vehicle took them back to the golf club. They pulled into the car park with its over-tended lines of vegetation. Bradley was poring over his notebook, as always, like a spy charged with memorizing state secrets. The Fixer conversed with the driver in Arabic; the driver was gesturing, with chagrin, at the lack of spaces.

'It's a lot fuller than yesterday,' Tim murmured.

'Naturally,' said Ruth.

'Because of the . . . because of what happened? Is it press?'

'No – they're here because it's Friday.'

As he and the Fixer began to unload the camera-bags from the boot, Miles mimed drinking with a certain wistfulness.

'How do they get home, if they're getting hammered?'

The Fixer raised his eyebrows amusedly. 'The wealthy ones have someone to drive them. The other ones just drive drunk.'

The cars they passed gave the impression of having been bought because they were expensive, like Christian Roper's shirts, or Raf's shades, and as usual Tim felt the inner double take provoked by the thought of his colleague. Was any new evidence being dissected online? Did the internet commentators have opinions, already, about the incident here yesterday? Tim wanted to know, almost as much as he wanted not to.

The bar was host to far more activity than yesterday. As Miles and his crew began setting up a place for Jason to conduct his online interviews, the throb of noise was already building. Elaine bustled in like an angry insect, talking to Jo, who tried to place a hand on the agent's arm but was rebuffed. Tim found himself being forced to listen to a group of British and Australian men in their forties, who had marked out their camp with bottles of champagne arranged like traffic bollards across a table. The group was alternating between work talk and remarks aimed at a polite, embarrassed waiter.

'Shut up, Keith.'

'I'm on the money. We'll ask this guy. My man! Sheikh Mo books a separate plane seat for his falcon – that's true, isn't it?'

'Won't be able to afford a plane seat for *himself* if this continues.'

'Storm in a tea-cup, mate.'

'It's a big tea-cup. Buyers are dropping out like fucking rats off a, off a . . .'

'Not here. Not Dubai.'

'Everywhere. It's just hit over there first. It's the whole world, mate.'

'Dubai's not in the world. My man! I'm right, aren't I? About the falcon? What's your name?'

The waiter responded neither with the slightly haunted look Tim had sometimes seen in Dubai's service industry, nor with the glazed servility that was more common, but – and Tim only saw it for a flash – with a kind of double-face, suggesting someone simultaneously cowed by, and dependent on, the people he spent all his time with. Tim adopted a studiedly pleasant tone as he set himself to the task of trying to book plane tickets.

'Is there internet anywhere here?'

'Yes, sir. Are you a member of the club?'

With a gumption Tim would probably not find in more comfortable circumstances, he tried his luck.

'No, but is there anywhere I could get on a computer – just quickly – without being a member?'

He saw the waiter make a brief calculation, his brown eyes narrowing; the gambit had been successful. 'If you go to Business Facility, sir. Past Relaxation Room and Legends' Enclosure and then on the left you will see it. You can use the password "GregNorman", sir, all one word.'

'Greg Norman, like the golfer?'

'No, sir: he spells it with two words.'

Tim tried to convey his gratitude, but the man was already halfway to helping someone else; he had moved away as if this tiny, irrelevant moment of collusion were a pivotal moment in a spy thriller. But then, Tim reminded himself, he didn't know what it might cost someone who worked here to flout the rules, even marginally. He thought of Ashraf – whom, it was almost certain, he would never meet again – and hurried into the corridor.

The walls were hung with photos of golfers. One huge, autographed black-and-white shot showed six men wildly celebrating some unknown victory. He went, as he was instructed, beyond the Relaxation Room and past the empty 'Legends' Enclosure', which seemed to be a premium version of the main lounge, with an elaborately stocked bar and an assembly of leather armchairs awaiting the presence of whatever legendary figures might appear.

But after this he did not, as the waiter had promised, 'see it on the left'. The corridor did snake around to the left, taking him back towards the main entrance and car park, but then – as if this had been a decoy – it curved back right, leading into the depths of the building. Tim retreated, looking more carefully this time for store cupboards like the one yesterday, which might yield a strange hidden room. He walked back as far as the Relaxation Room and tried another branch of the corridor, around another corner.

This is completely out of character, he thought irritably even as he continued to do it: throwing himself at one route and another, not making proper mental notes. It was the opposite of how he'd always approached things, since the days of school orienteering. He had a memory of being in a wood, during a weekend's training with older kids who took orienteering too seriously; trying to hold back a nosebleed as cold air numbed his face and the muddy ground sucked at his shoes. He'd forced himself to eliminate all the paths already taken, as they'd been trained to do, till only one was left. This hard-won triumph had remained in his brain as a sort of general exemplum. If you went, mentally, from one step to another, the world would make sense.

But this corridor did not even seem to lead back the same way it had first brought him. He had the same feeling he'd experienced in the mall, that he was playing some sort of computer game in which he caused the environment to change by walking around it. Of course, this was nonsense; Tim was annoyed at himself even for thinking it. Come on, he urged himself, as the air-con breathed its way into his consciousness. You could find your way round this place in your sleep. There have just been a lot of unfamiliar places, over here, in quick succession. And a lot of information that doesn't stack up, a lot of words that don't quite mean what they say.

He was back at the Relaxation Room, only a little way from the lounge where everyone else was; he could hear the chatter again, the expats' laughter; and now here it was, a white door clearly marked: Business Facility. It was just to the left, exactly where the man had said it would be. Tim was convinced it had not been there a moment ago. He would have sworn it.

The computers were of the blocky, nineties kind, and they sat on chunky, shiny oak cabinets: the whole room might not have been used since it was built. Still, when Tim brushed the mouse, the PC sprang into life as if it had only been waiting for him all this time. The password took him onto the net; he found a site with flight offers. For five hundred pounds he could fly back to Heathrow in the early hours of tomorrow morning. Five hundred pounds was a lot, but he'd get it back from Vortex. Tim felt his confidence rise a little. It didn't even matter if it pissed Vortex off. Being a good employee, winning Stan's approval, did not seem the important considerations that they once had.

I'll book it right now, he told himself, and navigated a series of pages, assuring the interface that he only needed a one-way ticket, that he would not need to book a hotel or hire a car once in London, that he would rather not receive information from the airline, the travel site, or any of their specially selected partners. He inputted his debit card details and waited for the moment of confirmation, the moment that would draw a line under everything: I am leaving tomorrow. I am out of here.

Instead of this, an exclamation mark and accompanying message informed Tim that his card had been declined. He was asked to check the details he'd entered. He typed them again, more slowly to eliminate any chance of error. Tim knew he was a long way from reaching his overdraft, there was plenty in the account – in fact the bank often got in touch imploring him to borrow more money, or take extra cards. He clicked to send through this latest version of the card details; again, the webpage was unmoved, and went so far as to warn him that a third unsuccessful attempt would lead to his being blocked from the site for an hour.

He found another site offering tickets on the same flight; put in the details again; the same thing happened. He brought his fist down heavily on the keyboard, twice, then immediately glanced behind him to see if anyone had witnessed it. You could probably get thrown out of the club for that, he thought – but actually, that would be OK. That would be fine. The computer emitted a low, mildly reproachful noise in response to his attack. Tim shut the computer window and left the room. He'd have to call the bank. Call the bank and then go back online for the plane tickets. Call, then get online, then get to the airport, then get away from this place.

Ruth was pacing the corridor when he returned to the lounge, and for a second it occurred to Tim that his absence might have been noticed, even held things up; but no, her attention was on someone else. 'You haven't seen Christian?'

'Christian? No.'

'He's literally vanished into the fucking air.'

'What's happening?'

'They're nearly ready to start with the to-camera bits. It's just, Jason's being funny about the script. Doesn't want to start till his agent approves it. She's bickering with Jo about whether we can go out on the course. It's basically a—'

'A shit sandwich?'

She gave him a reluctant grin. 'Exactly.'

'Why do you think Jason is being weird about reading the script?' Tim found himself asking, before he could stop. 'About reading? I mean, he's always doing this sort of thing.'

Ruth's eyes, a sort of sleepy green, fixed hard on Tim's. With a fizz of excited fear he realized that his conjecture was right, that Jason couldn't read; also, that Ruth already knew, and it was debatable whether he should have mentioned it.

'Will you go and look in the bathroom for me?'

'For Christian?'

Ruth snorted. 'Well, look for whatever you want in there, but yeah, I was thinking for Christian.'

A man in uniform was standing in the gents': as Tim approached, he pointed helpfully to the urinals, as if otherwise Tim might lose heart and leave again. Tim stood dutifully at the urinal. The cubicles were all unoccupied, and nobody else was here. On the side of the next urinal was a sticker: HOW ARE THESE FACILITIES? Where had he seen this message before? In Streng's trailer, of course. Tim's brain was connecting dots with other dots. He remembered the burn on his cheeks when Raf reprimanded him, in the most public way he could, for going into that trailer. In that instant, he'd wished any harm on Raf that there could be. Without even knowing it, he had wished it.

There was the dream. Why was it so vivid, his memory of strangling Raf? Why did he dream of Raf saying that he 'knew what was coming'? The chalet door had been open when Tim woke up; who opened it? Tim swung across planes of memory, back to the orienteering trip. He remembered coming home, sodden and exhausted, slumping down next to the fire in the grate, in the plodding comfort of the living room. Mr and Mrs Callaghan were watching some Sunday-night detective thing, one with hilariously ill-paired sleuths whose tetchy relationship is the very thing that leads them to a solution. And that had been the solution to the seemingly impossible puzzle: the culprit had been sleepwalking. 'That couldn't happen, could it, Henry?' asked Mrs Callaghan, and Tim's father, who had once worked in a pathologist's office, remarked mildly that he did think he'd heard of a case like that. 'In America, probably. Pretty much anything can happen in America.'

Tim felt needles of nausea jostling inside him. He stepped away from the urinal as two of the drinkers from the bar entered, exchanging witticisms. 'Something a little bit gay about this . . .' one of them began. They made no impression on Tim; he didn't even notice their faces.

He tried to rearrange his expression as Jason Streng appeared, for once without his agent, just outside the doors of the main lounge. On the other side of the doors, the noise was steadily increasing. Tim rolled his eyes at Jason with attempted insouciance.

'Any sign of progress?'

'It's not happening, mate.' Jason shrugged with vague regret: everything about his body language, Tim thought, suggested that in less than a week he would be by a pool, somewhere very far from here. 'The management won't let me go back on set till they've done proper safety checks on the cameras. I can do the internet bits, but at this rate we're going to end up bailing after that.'

'I'm going home myself,' said Tim, but even saying it reminded him that he had failed to clear the obstacles that prevented this from being a reality. He went into the members' lounge and immediately wished he had stayed outside. There were more people here, now: it felt like too many. The little gang of expats had swelled into a tribe who occupied four tables and had ordered an extraordinarily large bottle of champagne. Two waiters carried it between them and its arrival provoked a seeming pride around the tables, as if the drinkers were fishermen in the Dubai of old who had reeled in a giant catch. The drinkers had struck up a football song he vaguely recognized from an ad. In the background, as if in mitigation of their rowdiness, a kind of mellow jazz had begun to play; this, too, he thought he'd heard on an ad.

'I didn't even know they made bottles like that,' Tim said.

'It's – they call it a Methuselah,' said Ruth. 'You can get one called a Balthazar which is twice the size. And then there's a bigger one *again* called – what's it called?'

'Nebuchadnezzar,' said the Fixer, whom neither of them had noticed there.

'That's right,' said Ruth. 'I've only ever once seen it ordered. Most places, they have it on the menu but it's a bluff. They want to be seen to have a great menu. The time I saw some-one order it, they had a, erm, what do you call it?'

'A . . . credit card?'

'A brass band. A band came out and played and the owner drove across from Abu Dhabi to celebrate with the guy who'd ordered it.'

'Where did they come from?'

'Who?'

'The band,' said Tim, 'how did they have a brass band ready? Did they just have them sitting there for years in case someone went for the Nebuchadnezzar?'

'Probably,' said Ruth. 'There's an oil guy who lives in

Jumeirah Beach who keeps a lion and a lion-tamer in case he ever wants to impress his mates or whatever. Pays, I think it's four hundred thousand a year as a retainer. But he's never used them yet. The lion-tamer just goes out and does other gigs.'

'I could get a brass band within half an hour,' muttered the Fixer.

Bradley, baseball cap in hand, had prepared the cameras on the veranda outside, since there was too much noise to shoot here. He was holding a cup of green tea little bigger than a thimble. 'We're almost ready for Jason,' he said. 'Let's at least get these web videos done. They can at least use these.'

'I don't know if this is . . .' Ruth began. 'I mean, I don't know if this whole campaign is ever going to . . .'

'I am not a guy who walks away from something,' said Bradley. 'That's not who I am.'

Tim went back into the corridor. There was even less point than ever in his being there. He needed to be somewhere else; somewhere that was neither outside, with the cloying heat, nor in here with the disintegrating project and the Friday drinkers, the people for whom all this was somehow normal. He remembered the library hidden behind the storeroom, though with the half-expectation that it would have vanished in the way the computer room had appeared. No: there was the door handle. Tim pushed it carefully and stepped inside, and there, in a dressing-gown, and with a decanter of port in front of him, sat Christian Roper. Tim cried out in surprise. Christian gave him a ghoulish smile. It was clear that he was drunk, and planning on becoming more so. A fuzz of chest-hair peeped through the gown, and his hair was matted with moisture as if he had recently emerged from the shower. Tim thought back to that first-night dinner, only a few days earlier, when Christian had had a sort of impregnability about him.

'Excuse my attire!' said Christian, his voice thick with drink. 'I have been in the so-called Relaxation Room. Every-one needs to relax, don't they? Take a seat, take a seat.'

Not knowing what to do, Tim accepted the invitation, glancing around the untouched volumes and the arrayed portraits so as not to make eye contact. Christian made a show of offering him a glass of port; Tim was halfway to declining when it was poured out anyway. They sat there, in this film set of a room, like Victorian noblemen about to play a parlour game.

'Is it . . . is the campaign going to be shelved?' asked Tim.

Christian studied the table as if the question had not been asked, then answered it just as Tim was trying to frame another.

'I think it is fair to say,' said Christian with a reprise of the ghastly smile, 'that things are going to be somewhat stalled, yes. What with the camera falling. The death of the producer.

The, everything falling completely into . . .' He seemed to search for a phrase that would fit this construction, then abandon the effort. Tim, now used to dealing with Ruth, had to restrain himself from suggesting one. Instead, with a gathering of courage, he asked: 'I don't suppose you could help me to – to rearrange my flights?'

Christian laughed bitterly. 'I don't suppose you could get *me* out of here?'

It was hard to know what to say to that. Tim sensed that, in fact, no response was required: Christian, to judge from the series of breaths he took and the clearing of his throat, was preparing one of his speeches. Tim glanced over his shoulder. He wished somebody else would come in.

'You know, we set up in Dubai because I thought we could make most money that way. Not for ourselves. For the cause. For the people who need it. For the deficit of hundreds of millions of pounds that separates the poor from the rich. And you know? We did make money. We did pass on profits. I mean, we changed lives.'

'That's great,' said Tim, but Christian seemed not to hear.

'We bought a lot of property here,' Christian went on. 'It was guaranteed profit. You didn't need money; you bought with any kind of mortgage you could get, and sold it straight on. We . . . I mean, it was all about doing good. There's so much inequality. There's people dying one a second.' He gestured at his port glass as if somehow it exemplified the problem. 'You can never win,' he added. 'No matter what you do, there's more to do. There's always more to do. Always more.'

'But at least this ad,' Tim began. 'I mean, at least you're raising awareness . . .' he tailed off, sounding disappointing even to his own ears.

'Awareness,' Christian repeated, with an ironic nod. After another unpleasant pause, he went on. 'The money's just gone,' said Christian. 'It . . . it was never really there. And now the bluff's been called. Did you fuck my wife, by the way?'

Tim felt as if his intestines were being squeezed by a huge fist, one that had reached right into him. 'No,' he managed to say.

'Anything happen at all?'

'Nothing,' said Tim, hesitating just long enough to look guilty. 'Well, I mean . . .'

'I know she does this stuff,' said Christian, pitching, it seemed, to an invisible audience against the back wall. 'I know it's happened. I mean, I don't blame her. It happened with Raf. She gets bored. I'm all about . . . about the cause. To the exclusion of everything else. I wanted things to be all right, for everyone. I actually thought I could make things all right for everyone. Don't ever try and do that.'

Tim tried and failed to think of a response.

'I don't blame her,' Christian repeated.

He lowered his head. Tim looked at the fuzz of black hair on Christian's chest, some of it greying.

'I think I should go and . . . go and let them know where you are,' said Tim, rising from his seat. Christian nodded wryly and raised a hand. His eyes continued darting around the room, as if searching for some safe space to focus on, a place that did not exist.

Tim's phone was pressed against his ear. He was walking up and down a footpath which snaked alongside a hilly section of the course. A bark of laughter came through the still air: a golfer's quip, a conversation lighter and happier than his internal one.

It has not been possible to connect your call, said a voice in a computer-made fusion of real accents. *Please try again later.*

Why has it not been possible? thought Tim. How hard can it be for me to call my bank? The grievance felt like a feeble one, because of course, he had only the flimsiest idea how telephones worked; how computers, the internet, all the things he depended on actually functioned. The sun cut through his shirt with so little effort that he could almost picture it shredded, flapping uselessly like a tarpaulin. A single cloud shuffled rather pathetically towards the sun, like a lone soldier dispatched to stop a tank. Tim tried the number again; once more, the non-person commiserated with him and suggested he try his luck some other time.

It might be pointless to ask why there was a connection problem, but every other question led to a different question, which led in turn to a blank space. Who had pushed that camera off the gantry, if anyone had? Who were the people kissing outside Raf's chalet? Was the leaking of that information the real reason that Ashraf was fired? Was there any way that Tim himself could have done something in his sleep, with terrible consequences? At the fourth attempt he got through to his bank and was asked for an eleven-digit code, which, he was fairly sure, he'd never known.

'If you don't know the code,' said the cheery Scottish man on the other end of the line, 'perhaps you could give me details of any recent transactions?'

Tim struggled to recall anything he'd actually spent money on; minibar items, food, even the taxi ride had been billed to his room, and so were theoretical expenses at this stage. 'It's a bit odd, because I'm in Dubai,' he said, 'but I really need access to my card, because—'

'Dubai!' said the Scot. 'I've not been there. Very clean, I hear.'

'It is,' Tim agreed. He managed to summon the memory of the last things he'd bought with the card – all at Heathrow, before the flight – and the warm-voiced operative told him that they would look into things and hoped to be able to call him back within the same business day.

Tim stood in the heat. Jason was out on the veranda, methodically reciting lines for the website; Tim could just hear Bradley calling 'action!' and 'cut!' as he had done on the first day. Perhaps, as Bradley had said, they'd still be able to use these bits and pieces, even if the TV campaign never aired. That was something, he supposed. But the project didn't feel like it had anything to do with Tim any more, if it ever had.

Tim walked around to the front of the building, where he had been invited into Streng's car the day before. He had made a note of Rod's new number on his phone. What was there to lose? Tim dialled the number and, although it seemed as improbable as it had the first time, his brother answered almost immediately.

'What's up?'

'Were you asleep?'

'No,' said Rod, 'I've been having difficulty sleeping.'

'Maybe you should try staying awake during the day and sleeping at night?'

'Maybe,' Rod conceded, 'I've heard people do that. Are you all right out there?'

'Not really. No.'

Tim began to describe the difficulty of booking a flight

home, the frozen debit card, the way nobody was able to help. Rod, thousands of miles away, chewed this over.

'Just show up at the airport, mate. They'll have unblocked your card by the time the plane actually goes, surely.'

'But I won't have booked a flight.'

'It doesn't matter. Go to the airport. You can always get on a flight if you have money. Go to the desk and just pay for it there and then.'

It occurred to Tim he had been so thrown by the card problem, and by his various struggles with the internet, that he'd forgotten it was possible to buy things in the way people used to: by going to the relevant place and asking for it. 'But what if the card still doesn't work?'

'Then you call me and I'll do it on my card over the phone.'

'Have you got the money?'

'I've got plenty of money, mate. It might not be worth much in a couple of weeks' time, but we can get you out of Dubai. Just don't go there again.'

'I won't.' Tim had to swallow to ward off a wave of sentiment which rose in his throat and threatened to shake his voice. 'Thanks.'

He went back to the lounge. Even before he was through the door, it was obvious that something was happening: it was a tension in the air, a quiet alarm disturbing the composed faces of the waiting staff. Jazz was still playing over the speakers, but the ambient noise felt as if it had been sucked in, forced back inside the people making it; what was left was a sort of troubled hum. As Tim found a space near the doors, Miles gave him a warning wink and a thumbs-down. Two men were standing in mutual hostility, arms folded, and everyone else – he realized – had become an audience.

'I don't know what you want,' Christian Roper said, thrusting a finger towards Adam, 'but it seems like you won't be happy till you've run us into the ground.'

'You've run *yourself* into the ground,' said Adam. 'You can threaten me as much as you like.'

'I didn't chuck that fucking camera at you,' said Christian, 'but I wish I had.' Jo was on her feet now, coming to Christian's side, trying to pull him away. She said something to him in an urgent whisper. Adam was holding a recording device out in front of him.

'Will you admit,' asked Adam, 'that none of the money you make from this ad – from public donations – will go anywhere near the developing world, because you need it to bail yourselves out?'

It felt as if everyone in the room was waiting for Christian to refute this, but nobody really appeared to expect it. A look passed between the Ropers like collaborators running out of time. Christian spread his arms in what was probably meant to look like defiance.

'You think it's easy doing this? You think you could just rock up and wave a wand and poverty would disappear?'

'It's not about whether I can do it,' said Adam. 'It's about whether you can. I'm suggesting you can't. That you can't do what you're claiming to do.'

Jo's eyes appealed to the Fixer for help. The Fixer, without drawing attention to himself, began moving stealthily towards his employer. Christian gave a mirthless laugh like the ones he'd produced in the Relaxation Room.

'*You* don't do anything at all. You're a journalist. You just sit and fucking write. You don't make a contribution to the world. You just sneer at people who do.'

'Your contribution—' Adam began.

'I've made – do you know how much money I've made for charity?' Christian glanced around the room, at his helpless audience, and then struck himself with fake merriment on the chest. '*I* don't even know. I don't even know myself! It's off the scale!'

'Christian,' said Adam, 'I'm not—'

'Don't use my fucking name,' snarled Christian, and Tim wondered what alternative to someone's name there was, and had another memory of Roper as he'd been when this began: sitting clean-shaven in his kitchen, surrounded by well-arranged kitchenware, the letters MBE almost visible in a halo above his head.

'*Mr Roper*,' said Adam with cheerful irony, 'I'm not disputing that you have done amazing things. I'm saying that you have lost a lot of cash here, on things like Pearl that aren't going to be finished in a hundred years, and that this ad campaign is about trying to recoup—'

'I'm going to give you ten seconds to shut the fuck up,' said Christian.

'Christian . . .' appealed Jo. The Fixer was at Christian's shoulder like a political aide about to steer him away. Adam stood his ground; in fact, Tim thought, it was as if he was expanding, swelling up with his sheer sense of rightness.

'Or what?' asked Adam, with a theatrical spread of his arms. 'Or what happened to Raf will happen to me?'

Christian took a step towards the journalist. The Fixer put his hand on his collar. 'Get off me,' Christian said.

'We need to go,' said the Fixer.

'Saved by the bidoon!' crowed Adam.

The Fixer punched Adam hard in the face. Adam staggered back against the bar with both hands over his mouth, and a trickle of red came between his bunched fingers. A waiter, with a silver cloche on a tray bound for the expats, stood and gaped. A strange noise rose from the drinkers, a cry that began as glee and faded away. The moment had felt oddly banal, compared with the movie violence that was Tim's only reference point; there was none of the vicarious excitement or exoticism. Adam was asking at the bar for napkins. Christian stood absolutely still. The Fixer, seizing Christian by the arm, walked rapidly towards Tim and Ruth.

'It's time to leave,' said the Fixer.

'We don't have the cars booked.'

'I will have a car here in three minutes.'

'Take us with you,' said Ruth.

Tim tried to arrange his face as if he was indifferent to this prospect.

The Fixer shrugged and continued on his way, Christian hanging from his arm in defeat. Ruth looked at Tim and turned to go after them. Tim followed the ragged party out into the car park. He glanced back to see if Jo was coming after her husband, but she did not emerge.

An SUV, with shaded windows, was waiting for them. The driver was the same one who'd collected them from the airport. He put the radio on; the song was 'Killer Queen'. Nobody spoke. They drove in the dark.

The car dropped Tim and Ruth at the front of the Centrepiece. Christian was smiling in a detached way, like a candidate convincingly beaten in an election, as if to say that things were beyond his control now.

'Shall we go down to the beach?' said Ruth.

The sky was transitioning from light blue to a deeper one,

and the nightspots were coming to life; a waiter ushered a couple to an early-dinner table. It was like any other night. On the private beach, the sun-loungers were mostly retired for the day, though on one a woman in a peach-coloured swimsuit still slept, a John Grisham paperback resting on her belly. A man in a green T-shirt was smoothing down the sand with a rake. A preview version of the moon was on show in the corner of the sky, and a few tentative stars.

'What's a bidoon?' Tim asked, breaking a silence which had felt full of relief, or at least of resignation.

'It's what they call someone who doesn't have citizenship. Stateless people.'

'The Fixer doesn't have citizenship?'

'No. He'll be Iraqi or Kuwaiti. But part of a tribe which isn't recognized as being, erm, officially human. So they aren't able to work here, legally.'

'I remember Ashraf saying that word when he left. Or trying to say it; I couldn't work out what the word was.'

'It'll have come out, during the police investigation, that he was a non-citizen. A bidoon. And that's why he was fired. They don't have any rights, really. They just live on the run.'

'So, the Fixer . . .'

'He'll disappear for a little bit and then come back with a different identity. That's what people do here. Do you want a beer?'

'The Girl From Ipanema' was playing from speakers as they sat at a table. The waiter enquired as to the success of their stay so far. He asked the same question of a couple at the next table: a young Malaysian girl and a gentleman perhaps three times her age. When they reached out for their beers, Tim and Ruth's fingers met across the table for a second.

'So you're going in the morning,' she said.

'Yes. In the early hours.' The new song was 'Can't Take My Eyes Off You'. Tim felt the too-familiar words drift through his brain without landing. 'Will you go . . . what will you do? Go back to the States?'

She nodded; it looked as if her mind was somewhere else. She drank a gulp of the beer and ran her hand over her mouth. 'Back to the States, yes. What I'll do, I don't know. I'll wait for another thing like this to come up.'

'I've been thinking about maybe reassessing,' said Tim. 'I'm not sure this is exactly what I should be doing.'

'Well, this isn't an illustrative case. I mean, you're not normally going to deal with someone dying and the client plunging towards bankruptcy within three days of getting there.'

'No,' Tim acknowledged. 'But just in some more fundamental way. I feel like I need to do something that isn't just moving words around to try and convince people to buy stuff.

In fact, it's not even about buying stuff. It's more the idea of telling stories, creating this whole world which . . .'

'Which doesn't actually exist.'

'Yes. "A place where normal laws do not apply." That's Vortex's thing. After being here I sort of feel that normal laws might not be such a bad idea.'

'Is that what the word "vortex" even means?'

'I've never really thought about it. I mean, I assume so.'

'I don't think it does, if you look it up. Doesn't it mean a, like a, what's the word . . .?'

Tim grinned. 'I'm not sure I'm up to one of these.'

Ruth returned his smile. Her cheeks were a little pink, he noticed. 'A whirlpool. That sort of thing. A whirlwind.'

They ordered more beers, and time which had felt so thick and sludgy ever since Raf's death, now seemed to be whisking Tim towards the finish line. There was, all of a sudden, no real pressure to do anything; no expectation. For the first time since the very start of the trip, Tim could appreciate how it felt to be here as a tourist, how gloriously free everyone was of all obligations but to find the maximum possible luxury. He looked across to the couple, who were holding hands across the table: the girl was filling out a satisfaction questionnaire, the man correcting her, the two of them breaking out in happy laughs. There was laughter from other tables too: not the threatening cackles of the golf club, but a soft sound, a sound that meant togetherness.

Along the water, at the end of its walkway, the Burj Al Arab peered at them, a vertical line of little lights playing on-off-on-off; it reminded Tim more than ever of a recently arrived spacecraft. As they watched, a limousine crept down the walkway and passed the checkpoint, and two distant figures got out and were admitted to the hotel. The sight of them momentarily summoned in Tim a sense of adventures about to be had, strange and exciting things about to happen, and he experienced a sheepish plunge of regret that he would be getting on a plane in a handful of hours; that this pageant of leisure would all go on again and again without him.

'What are you thinking about?' asked Ruth.

'I was just thinking that it's kind of a shame to be going,' Tim confessed. 'Which is stupid, because I've been desperate to leave.'

'I think it's kind of a shame you're going, too,' said Ruth, looking the other way.

Tim cleared his throat. 'I . . . I mean, obviously we'll stay in touch.'

Ruth smiled rather sadly: it wasn't exactly that she was humouring him, Tim felt, but all the same, she knew better. If he thought about it, he too could probably foresee the gradual process over which they would vow to stay in touch, do so for a while in increasingly widely spaced emails, and end up floating impotently in each other's contact lists, now and again trading group invites to events the other could never attend.

'I suppose you've had this conversation with a lot of people before,' he pre-empted her, 'and it doesn't generally work out that way.'

'It's partly my own fault,' said Ruth. 'I tend to keep a low profile. I'm not big on, erm, on maintaining contact. I move around a lot.'

'Have you always?'

'Pretty much. We moved from Ireland to Brooklyn when I was eight, so I've always kind of felt that was just what you do. I thought my parents were crazy. I said: I'm not going to America. I've all my friends here.' She sounded very Irish, Tim thought, as the memory surfaced. 'To teach me a lesson, they drove off and left me standing there and for two minutes I believed I was going to be left living on my own. I started crying and the taxi came round the bend and scooped me up.'

'God,' said Tim, 'I don't think my parents would ever have done something like that. My mum didn't even like us going down the road without an escort.'

'My dad worked for a haulage company. He wasn't what you'd call the sentimental kind.'

He was enjoying the sound of her voice, and, when it was

229

his turn to speak, the seriousness of her narrowed eyes as she listened. Ruth ordered cocktails while Tim was in the toilet; then, when she went, he reciprocated. They played another couple of rounds of this game, deliberately choosing the most luridly coloured, the most crassly named drinks. Music painted the air from all corners now; they heard the singer from the first night starting up 'The Greatest Love of All', the forced emoting, the trickle of applause from those in earshot. Tim wondered briefly what had happened to the others, but the question did not feel like an urgent one. It was ten o'clock; he'd be gone in six hours, and, if all went well, on a plane in another two.

Their chat now was of a loose, unstructured kind, subjects superseding each other rather than following naturally. Ruth talked a little more about her family. Tim told her about Rod, then about the night he woke up with the nosebleed, the dream of killing Raf. It was the first time either of them had mentioned the tragedy, or even thought about it, for hours. Before too long it would be possible to go a day without thinking about it, impossible as it might have seemed at first; then it would be a week, and those gaps would stretch more and more over time.

'Well, it's a hell of a theory,' said Ruth, 'but how would you have gotten into Raf's chalet?'

'True. Maybe it is as simple as an overdose, after all.'

They discussed other aspects of the situation that might, or might not, be connected. It was true about Streng's inability to read, Ruth said. 'I knew you'd worked it out, but by yesterday I was too paranoid to say anything to anyone.'

'You could have trusted me,' said Tim, aware at last of being drunk, enjoyably so. 'I always thought we got on.'

'Me too,' said Ruth. 'But then I thought, you're just one of those guys; you're like that with everyone.'

'You mean, with Jo?'

Ruth shrugged. Tim fidgeted, wondering what to say.

'No offence, but you were wasting your time thinking you had something special with her. That woman will do anything to break up the boredom.'

There was a pause; Ruth seemed to regret saying it, although Tim felt it was reasonable enough.

'I don't really know what I'm doing,' he said, 'when it comes to this kind of thing.' He told her about Naomi and the unceremonious way things had ended.

'It's too bad,' said Ruth. 'Now you'll think of NYC as the city of romantic failures. Although maybe that's accurate.'

'You don't like New York? I thought you were looking forward to getting back there.' Tim realized he didn't want the present moment to end, and he was reluctant to hasten the next stage, the bitty sleep and airport trip and attempt to board a plane he was still not booked on.

'Oh, it's a great city. I just think people sentimentalize it. All the skating-on-the-Hudson. Carriage through Central Park. Movie stuff. It's just a place. It doesn't care about you any more than – well, than here. It just tricks people into thinking it's "their city", somehow. The same way Dubai is trying to.'

'I don't know if Dubai will ever be quite like New York,' said Tim.

'No,' said Ruth. 'It won't ever be quite like anywhere.'

It felt like a good final word, and without consultation they both stood up.

'I should start packing,' said Tim, and whether he meant it or not, it sounded like an invitation.

They walked away from the bar, up towards the Maritime Tower. At the top of the slope Tim turned for a last look at the Burj, the columns of lights like jewels along a suit of armour. He looked along the water at the vast wave of the Jumeirah Beach Hotel, every lighted window a life he knew nothing of. They walked past what had been their base, Ocean Chalets, the last place Raf Kavanagh had been alive. The feeling was stronger than ever that the whole of Dubai had been a mirage.

As they walked down the corridor Tim imagined Adam in the room a couple of doors down, writing up the story that

would finish WorldWise off: DRUNK ROPER SQUARES UP
TO REPORTER.

The green light blinked at them. Tim put the kettle on; he
went into the en-suite. When he came back, Ruth had got
under the covers and fired up the flat-screen TV.

'This is the second time I've gotten into your bed,' said
Ruth. 'I hope you don't start to get any ideas.'

On the TV, a handsome dark-complexioned man in a
skinny tie like those worn by lead singers was talking about
the financial markets. 'There's no doubt this could be as serious as the Wall Street Crash,' he was saying, with the same
barely concealed excitement the reporter had used to talk
about Raf's death the other day. 'There's no doubt this could
be absolutely catastrophic.'

'But how exactly did we get into this mess?' asked the
host, in a smooth BBC voice.

The financial expert gave a practised smile. He began to
talk about sub-prime mortgages and about equity and trust
funds. Tim got into the bed next to Ruth.

'Do you understand any of this?'

Ruth shut her eyes. 'I think,' she murmured, 'I think the
point is, erm, nothing makes any sense, nothing means anything. Is that basically what they're saying?'

'Yes, maybe.'

It was hard to tell who started it. Ruth felt very warm next to Tim. He rested his head on her chest, between her soft breasts. Thoughts had clogged up his brain over the past week, like a computer desktop slowed to trundling speed. Now as they moved together, he visualized the windows closing one at a time, disappearing. Raf's death, the crisis of the charity, the botched kiss with Jo, the mystery of the falling camera, the way things did not match up with their names, the way reality had fuzzed. There would be no revelation, no *Poirot* dénouement. He would go to the airport in a few hours and the game would be over. Until then, there was this; this was all that mattered.

PART THREE

PART THREE

12: A STORY

After we made love and before he shut his eyes, Tim made sure to set an alarm for the flight. Then he folded his clothes neatly and put them in his suitcase, and set out the ones he'd wear when he woke. He pulled on a pair of underpants, as if it was suddenly awkward to be naked with me. He went to sleep on his back. The past few days had been, as he Britishly put it, 'hard going'. In a few hours he would get up and go to the airport and we would never see each other again. So I lay there looking at him a little while.

Tim was right to suspect that the truth of Raf's death might disappear, be choked by all the phantom truths that grew over it like poison ivy. In Dubai, it can feel impossible to tell the difference between truth and replica; the next step from there is feeling like there isn't any difference. That everything fabricated is real, or the other way round.

One person can only see so much. Tim was an outsider. I had been here longer, I knew the protagonists much better.

And in the years since it all occurred I've been able to find out more. The people are as vivid to me now as when I was actually with them. Christian, the misfiring ideologue, outstripped by his own ambitions, clinging to money and property that weren't real, at a time when the world took a sudden and brutal audit of these things. Jo, frustrated and twitchy, sick of fundraisers, sick of being the trophy at yacht receptions and ambassadors' dinners, up to her ears in affairs, pinballing wildly between fitness regimes and drug habits. The Fixer, living in the margins, a man who could arrange anything except a legal existence for himself. Bradley, work-obsessed, perhaps in denial about his sexuality. Miles, a cameraman both strong and smart enough to push a camera off a gantry in such a way as to avoid killing anyone. A star terrified of his secret getting out, and an agent infected by that terror.

Then there was Raf, and me. Before we go any further, there are a few things you should know.

When I was seventeen I went to prom. It wasn't our year yet; someone knew someone and we got a group invite. The condition of entry was that you had to dress up and flirt. I wore red lipstick and a ballgown made for a Barbie doll which barely came down to my knees. There was a boy called Ryan with very green eyes. 'Your hair is fucking amazing,' he said. He told me his family came from Ireland; people were always claiming that. We went back to a house party; had rum and Coke. I wasn't used to drinking, but I acted as if I was. I lost my friends. He took me up to his room and I remember thinking: well, this is what you hear about. We had sex three times and a few weeks later I threw up in the shower.

Not having the baby was so far out of the question, there wasn't even a question. Abortion was legal where we lived, but it was illegal in Ireland, and our house was still emotionally part of Ireland. The only thing worse than having the baby, from my parents' perspective, would be getting rid of it. I would look at my body, lying in the bath, and wishful thinking would convince me that I couldn't feel the thing in there. There'd been a mistake. Or something had happened to it. It had disappeared the same baffling way it showed up. Then I'd feel guilty knowing how many people were desperate for a child and couldn't have one.

The weeks went by. At night I lay on my side, trying to get comfortable. I would hear the people in the next apartment having parties. The Ramones came through the wall, corks popped, college kids screamed with laughter. I was eighteen and all I could make out, in the long murk of those nights, was that I had signed away my life before it had begun.

He was born on a hot day. There was a black woman on the next bed who was having her sixth. 'What else am I gonna do w' my life?' she asked me. 'Be a goddam baseball player?' She was calling this one Texas; they were all named after states. In the delivery ward I could hear car horns blaring on the street below and feel the close, dirty heat of the air outside. They whisked him away before I even saw his face. They were measuring and weighing him for half an hour and I could hear him wailing. I begged them to bring him back.

'Don't worry, honey,' said one of the midwives, 'you'll be seeing him plenty.'

I called him Owen. Mam took him with a thin smile. Da patted him on the head and asked if he could smoke in the hospital.

He cried at night, he cried in the morning. He wouldn't feed properly but he was outraged if I took the breast away. I worked in a 7-Eleven and a RadioShack, I worked at a fried chicken place and came home stinking of grease. Mam looked after him; I spent all my time wondering if he was calling out for me. If I came home to the sound of him crying, it felt as if he must have been crying all the time I was away. I would argue with Mam while Da smoked out of the window.

The parties carried on next door. I went round in my nightie to ask them to be quiet, and people looked at me like I was fifty years old. Sometimes I couldn't raise the energy to take my clothes off before crawling into bed; some mornings

I couldn't get into the shower. I got fired from RadioShack for falling asleep at the cash register. I got fired from the 7-Eleven for calling a customer a cocksucker.

It didn't matter. There were more jobs. It wasn't like I wanted any specific job more than any other.

Owen started to smile. He learned to laugh and hold a little soft ball and reach out for his best toy, a panda called Lloyd. He started to crawl and make noises that could be 'mama'. Every milestone like this, even the stupid ones, felt like an achievement. That's why people are so boring about their kids. If you see a two-year-old say 'I have a stick' and the mother coos like it's the Bolshoi Ballet, you think parenting must have turned her brain to mush. But if you are that mother, that 'I have a stick' is the end of a timeline that started with something the size of a seed growing inside you, and went through a thousand diapers, a hundred hours of mashing up carrot, wiping juice off a chin, mopping up vomit, springing out of bed ten minutes after you got in, blanking the fuck-you looks of strangers on the plane. You don't get any praise for all that, and you don't expect it. 'I have a stick' is all you get. So it looks a lot bigger from where you're standing.

I got a job that gave me half a day off a week and went to a group called Thursday Moms, where we sat with our kids on our knees and sang songs and drank coffee. A couple of years ago it would have sounded appalling, but now I needed it. Most of the moms had good hair and nice dresses and they brought in healthy homemade snacks and knew all the words to the songs. They had taken time off from graphic design jobs or magazine columns and were easing back into work. They all knew my situation and they were studious in not mentioning it, generally by not talking to me. But there was a mother called Martha who looked almost as shitty as me. Her husband had gone off with a dancer. We became friends. She worked for a film producer.

'You should be a runner,' she said.

'Are you kidding? I'm too tired to even walk.'

'No. Like, a runner on set.'

One day, when Owen was two and we were taking him around the park, Mam reached out and touched his red cheek. 'He's a good boy, isn't he, now?'

'He's wonderful,' I said.

'We'll be away to Ireland soon, I think,' said Mam, as if it were a whimsical idea, something she'd just come up with. 'Da thinks it's time to go back. They're opening up a big new place in Dublin, his company. And your grandmother's not been well.'

'But I . . . I mean, he's so small,' I said. 'It would be a hell of an upheaval. Just when he's starting to know what's what.'

'Well, that's right,' Mam agreed.

A plane roared overhead and we both glanced up. When our eyes came to meet again, we both looked away.

'You know you can always come over, you can always bring him over,' she added, slipping her arm through mine for a second.

It was a relief to her, I thought; maybe it was a relief to both of us.

I enrolled Owen in preschool. He yelled and tugged my elbow and pleaded not to be left. I showed up at a shiny office for my first day as a runner with snot smeared down the sleeve of a twenty-dollar dress, the best thing I had to wear. My new boss asked me to get him a coffee. Then he asked me to go tell someone he'd see them in ten minutes. Then I had to get him another coffee, and then a bagel. That was all that happened on my first morning. I couldn't believe this was a job. I earned $2.30 an hour more than I used to at the 7-Eleven.

After two weeks I got a babysitter and went to a movie with Martha. She bought me a beer afterwards: my first drink in three years. When I got home, the babysitter said Owen had slept all the way through. I took Martha into his bedroom. He had Lloyd the panda clasped to his chest and he was smiling a little.

'He's freakin' lovely,' said Martha, beer on her breath. She squeezed my hand. I thought: I can do this. I have a life; not the life I imagined, but a life all the same.

I worked hard for the film producer. His name was Solomon Katz and all he generally wanted was for me to make him coffee, or pick up the phone and say he wasn't there. None of his various projects was ever likely to be made; his business was to secure funding for possible films which he then allowed to be shelved in order to pitch something else for more funding. He had the contacts to live as a movie producer without producing movies. I was a runner without having to do much running. It began to dawn on me that a lot of people's jobs consisted of nothing more than convincing someone else they were doing a job.

How do we get from here to Dubai? It's all the same story. Every story is somehow part of every other one.

About a month in, I picked up the phone and was halfway through explaining that Katz was away when I realized the call was for me. There was a problem at kindergarten. Owen was having trouble breathing. I ran in a daze to the subway, sprinted five blocks plastered in cold sweat. There was a doctor there. Owen was lying in a makeshift sickroom with an oxygen mask on. He looked like an evacuee child from one of those British war movies. His brown eyes asked me to help him: it was the first time ever I hadn't been able to. The doctor looked wryly at me.

'He's a lucky guy,' he said. 'He's had a bad allergic reaction.'

It was an anaphylactic shock, he said. Normally caused by traces of nut. The kindergarten's principal, Mandy, kept saying they'd never had anything like this, as if somehow that would comfort me. All I wanted was to take Owen home, but when I was alone with him, I was terrified in case it happened again. He slept in my bed and I held him next to me, putting a hand in front of his mouth every few minutes to feel his breath. I kept my eyes open all night and the night after that.

'I don't want to be sick like that again, Mom,' he said once.

'You won't be. You won't be.'

I took him to a doctor. I got every leaflet ever printed about nut allergy and intolerance. I became militant about checking ingredients. I cooked him the same four meals on rotation. Gradually it became normal. You can make almost anything seem normal through repetition.

He turned four, then five. Katz loaned me out to a buddy; I spent three days on an actual shoot, a TV movie about a contract killing. I learned the roles of a shoot: the hierarchy. The director, AD, producer, AP. The DOP. I loved it, talking in these codes like someone in the White House. I started looking for more freelance work on shoots, any shoot, anyplace. New York was crawling with them. At any given moment in the city, people were pretending to make love, hold up banks, die. If it was a weekend, I'd take Owen with me, set him up in a corner with his toy train. People would admire his big eyes and long eyelashes and say, 'Is he yours? He's a cutie! He's so beautiful!' Yes, I'd say, he's mine, and sure you can play with him, but please don't give him any snacks. Owen would solemnly explain the rules of the train game. I would watch from across the room, with that feeling in my chest, the willing surrender to love, to the slavery of it.

On one job I met a producer called Crawford Henry. A backwards name, as he said when introducing himself: it felt like a line he'd used a lot. I didn't mind. He was a little older than me; his parents were from the Caribbean. He had a loud, infectious laugh and his aftershave had a delicious smell which I instantly came to think of being his own. We went for a drink and he sat Owen on his lap and told him about how steam engines worked; we took Owen to the premiere of a kids' movie about penguins and Crawford arranged for Owen to meet one of the cast and try on a penguin costume. We saw each other for a few months. Nobody had touched me since that night of the party four years earlier. Crawford was gentle and he made me laugh. He was the one who pointed out how often I said 'erm' in the middle of a sentence. He and Owen called each other 'dude'.

One day he asked to see me on my own. It was winter and well below freezing. I got a babysitter. We walked across Brooklyn Bridge. There was a silver fuzz of skyscraper-light in the frozen water below us, and the buildings loomed like friendly listeners. In my memory it's just like the poster scene on the walls of the Ropers' apartment.

'I have to stop doing this,' said Crawford.

'Stop . . .?'

'Stop seeing you. I'm so sorry, Ruth, I really am.'

He was married; he lived upstate with his family. I was too numb to be angry. I allowed him to hold me at the entrance to the subway, with a panhandler cursing us for encroaching on his patch. Crawford walked away in his big tan coat. I went home in the cold and in the morning I told Owen that Crawford wouldn't be coming any more.

'Did he not want to be my dad?'

'What?'

'I thought he was going to be my dad.'

I was trying to get ready for work, make-up half on, clothes half on. 'It's not like that, honey. Your dad . . . we talked about this. Your dad went away, and—'

'But we could get a new one. I thought Crawford was the new one.'

'So did I.'

'Did I do something wrong?'

After that, I did no more dating. If I met someone and we slept together, or even started talking like we might sleep together, I would make a performance of saying that I had a child, so nothing serious could ever happen. That was generally enough to sabotage the romance. There were a couple of nice men who persisted, saying that they'd love to meet him, maybe we could all hang out together. But the more someone tried to accommodate the idea of Owen, the more prickly and impossible I became. His father had left, Crawford had left, even my parents had left. I wouldn't give anyone else the chance.

Owen was tall and freckled like me, with a fair mop of thick, loose hair which I never liked to let people cut. He was good at school, without standing out. At parent–teacher interviews I got favourable reports, and they never asked about his dad: a third of his class were from single-parent homes. Actually, the longer I went on, the less isolated I felt. I took Owen to friends' houses and met moms who were on their own, literally or effectively (because their husbands worked such long hours) or emotionally (because they hated their husbands). I was OK leaving Owen at his buddies'. Nowhere near thirty, I was assistant producer, once even producer, and my botched early years of adult life began to look like they could invert themselves into a kind of head-start.

Owen went away for a weekend with his friend's family – the O'Neills, good Irish blood – and then one summer on a four-day activity camp. I was left rattling around the apartment and yearning for my boy in a way that felt embarrassingly close to lovesickness. I called the camp two of the three nights and could sense his eye-rolling as I went through the questions neurotic mothers ask in TV movies: are you eating enough, who are you hanging out with, did you remember to tell them about the nut thing, even though I already sent a letter and called to make sure they got it?

Nine, ten, eleven. He was getting big enough that I could bring him on location shoots. He'd sit in the corner and read a Stephen King novel or beaver away on his own screenplays, writing in biro on A4 pads: *The Baker Who Went Crazy*, *The Little Leaguers Find Pirate Treasure*. Sometimes he'd run errands for the director and everyone would say what a cool kid he was. At night he slept in my bed and I would feel the warmth of his breath, admire his gangly limbs, manliness stealing across the still-childish features.

You'll be thinking: so what next? Why am I even hearing about this, unless there's a bitter end? Do me a favour and suspend that thought for a second. Leave me lying alongside the boy, already threatening to grow as tall as me, smelling a little like me, his long eyelashes fastening down his eyelids, his breath on my neck.

In 2000, Owen was fourteen. I was a seasoned producer with a long résumé, features and sitcoms mingled with infomercials. I could work on a studio floor or a film set. I had a cellphone. Martha had moved to LA; most of my other friends I barely saw. I was absorbed by the work and all my spare time was spent with Owen. We went to see the Yankees and got caught on the roving camera, flashed up on the big screen; I tried to make him hug me and got a play-punch instead. He was in a high-school production of *The Crucible*, playing the old judge, with pantyhose on and talcum powder to whiten his hair. He called me Hillary after Clinton, because he thought I spoke like her when I was trying to be authoritative; he left notes written in the style of a political aide.

H.

Gone to baseball practice and may check out a movie.

Will return circa 23:00 hours.

O.

I knew there would be girlfriends, or there already were. I rehearsed my cool-mom smile, my cooking of fun meals, my nonchalant attitude. I was confident of making a good impression on any girl I had to power-share with. I was a lot younger than they'd expect a mom to be. I could identify any Nirvana song; I had crushes on the male cast of *Friends*.

There was a job in LA that part-overlapped with spring break. I decided to take Owen out of school for the remaining days and we planned the trip like two sophomores. West Hollywood, Beverly Hills, the beach. We were going to stay with Martha and her kids while I was working. They got tickets to a Dodgers game; Martha even talked about driving them down to San Francisco and I started planning to extend the trip so I could go along.

It was United Airlines. I got us upgraded. Owen reclined his seat and sighed. 'Wow, your job is hard work.'

I said something sarcastic. Flying never really agreed with me, plus my period was due; I felt scratchy and on edge. I was planning to knock myself out with a Valium. An hour in, I took the pill and was halfway into the embrace of sleep – that warm feeling, like being wrapped up – when Owen nudged me.

'Hillary. Can I borrow a hundred bucks?'

'What?'

He was leafing through a catalogue of goods available at LAX. 'When we land, I want to buy this.'

The face of the watch was indigo, with silver hands and a button to switch to digital display; its design was 'ergonomic', a word I recognized from publicity materials, meaning pretty much nothing.

'That's a watch for . . . that's too old for you.'

'It's amazing.'

'I don't have three hundred dollars to spend on a watch.

And you certainly do not need to spend three hundred dollars on a watch.'

'Fucking hell,' he muttered.

'Don't talk to me like that.'

His lip curled, on the verge of some insolent comeback.

'And don't argue with me, Owen, I'm not in the mood.'

'For God's sake,' he said, shaking his head and angling himself away. I did the same, arching my body towards the window. We lay there, self-consciously sulking, and then the tablet kicked in and sent me to sleep.

Hands wrenched me out of darkness: urgent, clammy hands. I blinked a couple of times and the world was a sickly, over-colourful horror. People were standing in the aisle, looking worried. An air hostess was shaking me urgently. I felt a little sick. That was the order in which I logged my first impressions. Then, with a plunge of my stomach, Owen himself. His face was white; he was clinging to the handrest. I went cold.

'Owen, Jesus Christ.'

'He's having some kind of reaction . . .' the hostess began.

'He's allergic,' I said, or shouted; I could hear heads turning, activity stalling. 'He was meant to have the nut-free option.'

'We have him down for vegetarian,' said the hostess, straightening her skirt.

'He's nut-free,' I yelled, taking Owen's hand. It was limp as a handkerchief. Waves of panic tore at me. I wanted to rip off my clothes; I was hot as hell. I took him by the shoulder. With my other hand I was throwing things out of my handbag: my own medication, a pocket mirror, anything in the way of the antihistamines. I got one and crammed it into Owen's mouth. His lips puckered and he spat it out. I forced it back in.

'We need a doctor,' I screamed at the woman.

A doctor was already on the way, she said, from first class. Owen's face was going slack.

'Honey,' I shouted, 'just keep breathing, just keep breathing.'

'Help me, Mom,' he said out of the corner of his mouth. His eyes were glazing over. I felt as if everything below chest level had been hollowed out and replaced with ice. I stood up, even though the seatbelt sign was on; I thought I was going to vomit or shit myself.

'WE NEED A FUCKING DOCTOR.'

'A doctor will be right with you,' said the woman, as if I'd asked for a brandy.

Owen was gasping, clinging to the armrests.

'Why the fuck did you give him something with nuts in? Didn't he say?'

'He did say,' the air hostess told me, 'and I told him the vegetarian meal should be fine.'

'But it's not fine, is it? It's not fine!'

'A doctor will be right here,' she said again.

'Help me, Mom,' Owen begged again, barely audible. I squeezed his hands in mine. I kissed him on his damp cheek. Scenes from his fourteen years ran through my mind, not in the life-flashing-before-you way of movie sequences, but in a jumbled montage. He was filling the bathtub in one of our vacation motels, but the shower setting was on, and he soaked the room. He swung for a baseball, sent it flying out of the diamond, trotted around the bases and gave high-fives to the whole team. The little notes on the kitchen table, the Chinese takeouts, the sound of his voice on the phone from camp, the graduation day, wedding day, all the stuff that was ahead. And then the argument that had been the last conversation we held.

The doctor came. I had to get out of my seat. People were huddled in the gangways, where business met economy, watching furtively through the curtain. I was crying. The air hostess put a hand on my shoulder. The doctor was bent over Owen. He asked a crew member about releasing an oxygen mask. He asked if I was the mother.

'Help him!' I shrieked.

'I am trying to help him, ma'am.'

I stood in the aisle, my hands in my boy's hair, as the doctor leant over him, sweat collecting on his bare forehead.

It flashed across my mind that you heard about stuff like this happening, but normally as a great escape, a turning point. I swore to unknown gods that I would do anything if they'd save him. Owen tried to say something to me, his eyes rolling back to meet mine. He couldn't get any words out. The doctor was taking my arm. I shook it off. These are the events as they probably happened. Nothing is ever more accurate than 'probably'. When the really big stuff happens, we have to make up stories: the brain shrinks away from the details, like someone beaten back by a fire.

He was gone.

My parents flew over. Martha came to New York and stayed two weeks. The school held a fundraising concert. I received cards in the post from people I barely knew. It was in the *Times* and the *Post*. Lawyers made contact and offered their services. Could I prove I had registered him as nut-allergic? Yes, I could. One told me I could sue for hundreds of thousands. But I couldn't face courts, processes; I couldn't get out of bed. I settled out of court for a tenth of what we should have gotten. I didn't care. Money meant very little to me. What was I going to spend it on? No number corresponded to a version of reality in which my boy was alive. Nothing overruled the reality, the coldness of moving out of the apartment, Martha loading things into boxes and asking me to say yes or no to each item. She offered to move back to New York and be my roommate. I wanted her to, but couldn't accept: she had a husband, her own children. I moved into a one-room place. I kept working. As soon as I got home, I took a sleeping pill; as soon as I woke up, I went out. I automated myself. A doctor prescribed anti-depressants and I drove a wedge between myself and my feelings.

Some days, I laughed and drank with colleagues after we wrapped for the night. You would take me for someone who was going back to a happy house, maybe with a strapping husband, sleeves rolled up, dishing up rich-smelling food to an army of eager kids. Planning a summer camping vacation or welcoming parents for Thanksgiving. I could even take myself for that person. The narrative in which everything went right made more sense than the one I found myself in. I told people I'd never had children: had chosen not to, for work. Or that I was married with three of them. I could tell people what I wanted, because I rarely spoke to anyone twice. I moved through life like a rumour.

When he'd been gone nearly a year, I worked on a shoot in Hong Kong. The film featured three boys about sixteen: the age he nearly was, the age he wouldn't ever reach. It was a bad choice. In a hotel room designed to neutralize emotion, I found myself thumping on the window with my fists, trying to break it maybe, or just trying to express something that had no shape. The window didn't break, but somebody complained. A staff member came up and I shouted at them that my son was dead. The film's director was called to the room. He said maybe I should get therapy. He knew some-one. I said, why not?

Six months of bereavement counselling. Where over a dozen years before I'd spent Thursdays with people who had young children, I now spent them with people whose chil-dren had been taken away. We sat in a circle and discussed our 'stories'. One lady had had a son, about Owen's age, who had been abducted and killed and eventually dragged from the Hudson River. 'Every day,' she told us, 'I say: give him back. Give me back that brown-eyed boy.' I cried, but not for her. We were all locked in our individual suffering. When I spoke about what had happened to Owen, I could see people nodding, tilting their heads, switching off. I'd done it to them, too. We were all victims' mothers, like the caption on the newscast when I was interviewed. VICTIM'S MOTHER. It was the same thing in my individual counsel-ling sessions. 'People who've lost someone often find . . .' she would say. 'Mothers in your position feel . . .'

People were taking their kids swimming, having barbe-cues, tucking them up to sleep. I'd been one of them myself. If they heard what had happened to me, they'd say: how terrible. They would mean it, too – they weren't lying. But nor were they really telling the truth. They were just doing what you do when you hear a story. Owen only existed now as a story. That poor woman, they all thought, before something else caught their attention.

A job came up in Dubai. It was 2003 and I had been on my own three years. The client was a charity called WorldWise. I flew over and met Christian Roper. He was bracingly attractive, full of confidence: he already knew my history. He put an arm round me and told me how awful it was. I stayed in their spare room and Jo cooked great meals and walked around looking incredible, and then got off her face and slept with people. I stayed with them for two weeks. Halfway through the trip, they took me on a tour of the city. Christian talked about how they'd bought ten properties, flipped them, put the profits into the charity. Jo took me round a mall where they got everything for free by mentioning they were the Ropers. We went to a private beach and ordered lobster and champagne. On the last night they took me to the restaurant at the bottom of the Burj, surrounded three-sixty degrees by fish tanks. When I got home, I saw it was generally described in tourist guides as an 'underwater restaurant'. The Burj itself was only a 'seven-star hotel' because it had awarded itself seven stars and nobody could take them away. Here, you made stuff up, and it stuck.

Christian got me back to Dubai in 2005, to make one of a series of short films. The city was in an orgy of expansion: in every pause in conversation you heard the growling of construction vehicles. Everywhere were billboards about THE FUTURE. You could go from hotel to mall to cinema to party without seeing the sky. That sort of detachment from reality was what I needed. I went drinking with Christian and Jo. They often left separately. Once Christian tried his luck with me; he didn't seem offended when I said it was probably not for the best.

Christian had begun from a healthy standpoint. Having become rich, he wanted to redistribute his wealth for good. He bankrolled an entire village's modernization in Zambia: a new hospital, school, all the stuff pictured on WorldWise's walls. Yet for every new vaccination he paid for, there was a child screaming somewhere else; every time he signed up to pay for something, details of an even more urgent cause arrived in the mail next day. He couldn't mend the world all on his own, of course. But, Jo told me, he felt the world could heal itself. Could, and yet wouldn't. 'He started to rant on about why people were so indifferent to suffering. I said, well, make your own charity. And here we are.'

WorldWise was set up to exploit all the financial loopholes Dubai offered, as so many businesses had over the previous decade. The Ropers, like half the world's financial institutions, were gambling with huge sums in a place where official gambling was illegal. Unlike all the others, they were giving the winnings to the poor. Even so, they were in the same danger as all the others: if the game ever changed, they would hit the ground hard. At this time, nobody in the world predicted such a change, and certainly no one in Dubai. Brits, Americans, Russians came over and looted it like prospectors. They had three-day parties in the desert. They played golf and bought apartments. Everything was on credit. Money was what you said it was.

It suited me, this bubble. New York meant nothing to me now. I stayed on the move. The only reality I engaged with was minute to minute. This actor needs transportation. These crew hotels need booking. This will do some sort of good. Someone, somewhere in the world, will benefit from this.

Christian and I had come to a similar place by different routes: we both cared more about our projects, the abstracts, than about the people around us or even ourselves. I worked on small promotional shoots for him in East Africa and Brazil and then, in 2008, Dubai came round again. I went first to London to meet Raf Kavanagh. He'd been hired as producer and I as AP; this was an inversion of the way things should have been, looking at our respective levels of experience, but I was passive about status and even money these days. They had long since ceased to mean anything. 'I normally get on well with the people under me,' he said. He enquired after my age and grimaced in pity when it turned out I was forty. 'No husband?' he asked. No, I said. Again, the look of pity.

He took a phone call from a girl in the middle of our meeting and continued to text her after they'd hung up; he didn't make eye contact for the final twenty minutes. 'See you at the airport,' he said as a parting shot, and described some of the free things he'd been able to get on flights in the past.

A few days later we – and Tim, Miles and Bradley – all assembled on that grubby grey day at Heathrow, to make a commercial that would cost at least a million dollars. I was already aware that, unfortunately, WorldWise didn't have a million dollars any more. It had a bunch of properties that were theoretically worth far more than that. But the theory was coming to an end.

By the time Tim got the contract for the commercial, I'd picked up enough to know that Christian was in trouble. Dubai was still marketing itself as aggressively as ever, but the property expos were quiet, the resorts were half empty, and business owners were beginning to panic, while repeating loudly and desperately that they were not panicking and nobody else should either. The Fixer remarked in an email, a couple of weeks before we flew, that this new commercial was 'extremely inadvisable'. He was cheerful about it. We agreed that it was best to get on with it.

The signs of Christian's decline were the same as the signs of Dubai's: everything was going on like before, too much like before. He talked incessantly about 'a chance to make a difference', about how 'pumped' he was for the project. He had become a walking set of slogans. Jo, I noticed over the next couple of days, was more detached than when I had last been there, numbing everything with her strange combination of narcotics and the gym. She was ambling through life in Dubai like someone under anaesthetic, as a lot of people were. On top of this, there was the secrecy surrounding Jason Streng. There was low-level chaos to do with locations and ground staff because rumours were spreading that nobody would get paid. I decided to put my fingers in my ears. It would be a week and I'd move on to something else.

But working with Raf was enough to make that sort of indifference impossible; within a day or so, something about him had begun to shift the fog that had separated me from feeling for so long. He was astonishingly mannered and arrogant, all of it concealed by that untouchable quality that comes with good looks. Lighten up! I'm just having a laugh! He had come to Dubai to enjoy himself, the same way he might go to Vegas; the 'charity thing' was a detail so incidental he was capable of forgetting it altogether. During his couple of nights contributing to the fight against Western excess and injustice, he drank heavily and gobbled up drugs supplied by Jo. He was rude to everyone and treated me, in particular, like a maidservant. None of this alone would make anyone kill him, surely. But – as everyone knows – people murder for reasons they couldn't anticipate, even for reasons they aren't aware of themselves.

And there were certain triggers. There was the moment I dropped my bag on the first day and my stuff fell all over the floor, and out came a picture of Owen which I'd almost forgotten was in there: flushed and freckled, bright-eyed, running in a race at school sports day. Tim saw it briefly and I was filled with a longing to tell him everything, a longing that couldn't be indulged. He could only react one way to the story: my God, I'm so sorry. What was the use of collecting another set of condolences? But as I was trying to compose myself, in came Raf with one of his attacks on my work. It reminded me of the peremptory way he'd spoken to me on that first meeting; something hardened inside me.

Then on the way back to the hotel, the clincher, if there was a clincher: the discussion about the boy who choked to death because the ambulance couldn't find him. Raf whistling 'Where the Streets Have No Name'. Like the success of a single joke trumped the entirety of what came with a boy's death. It was so obscene, so outlandish, that a whole life could be cancelled out in this way by a one-liner from someone more fortunate. The obscenity made me feel, over the course of that evening, more and more rash – almost panicky, as if I had to do something to change it. As we all sat down in the restaurant, I looked up at the stars, painted in that beautiful, unreal way across the Dubai horizon. The injustice filled up my throat, threatening to make me gag, in a way I'd thought I was now immune to. Owen was not here with me, he would not be back in the chalet to cuddle up to. I would never see him again. And yet Raf was so far away from being affected by death that he could make that joke, and nobody really minded.

I heard him lead the conversation, as I lay on Tim's bed in the chalet, amid the jokes and chatter and drinking. I heard him tell the assembled team that charity was essentially pointless. A 'bottomless pit', he called it. His thesis: things were so fucked up that it was beyond our ability to improve them, and so we shouldn't even try. He had a point, of course. A lot of things weren't fair, and maybe the only answer was to hope you stayed on the right side of the universe's whims. But there are things we can alter. As I lay on that bed, I felt the culmination of this mental, or quasi-mental, process which had gathered up all the evidence and was imploring me to act, to alter just one thing.

The process had worked away in the core of me, silent and

stealthy as poison entering the bloodstream. Dubai shows that nothing is real, it said. Everything is a story. The charity itself is a story, so is the whole of this city; nothing is more substantial than a series of words, and words can mean anything. Owen dying in your arms is nothing more than an anecdote to Raf Kavanagh. Raf Kavanagh dying in your arms would be an anecdote to someone else.

I could have gone to sleep, and perhaps these thoughts would have dispersed by the morning. But I didn't go to sleep, as Tim did. I went quietly out, avoiding Miles on the floor. I left the door on the latch. The air was only just losing its warmth now; it had that spiciness to it, an invitation. I knocked on the door and heard him come shuffling. He was wearing only underpants, semi-sentient.

'To what do I owe the pleasure?' Raf slurred.

I felt nothing as coherent as avenging fury, or rightfulness; I felt as if I were following a set of instructions. I got onto the bed with him. 'Wow,' he said, indistinctly. 'I knew the bitch thing was a front. I knew you wanted it as soon as we met that first time.'

'And you . . .?' I said.

'I'm open to persuasion,' he mumbled.

I got on top of him. He shut his eyes. I slung him onto his front. He whispered something through sleep. I was straddling him, and I turned him and held his head and shoved it into the pillow. He started to struggle, but weakly. I was stronger than him, even without the drugs. He was wriggling a little. I held him down harder. It was incredible how easy it was. I felt his body go limp, by degrees; he was making a high-pitched whine like a guinea pig. There was a spreading warmth below us as he lost control of his bladder. No retreat from here.

I held him down until it was done. Then I dragged him, like a crash-test dummy, off the bed, across the floor, into the bathroom. Pushed him into the hot tub. Left his chalet and walked back across the compound. My heart was beating fast, but it was like the buzz from strenuous exercise, nothing more. Less than half an hour after leaving it, I was back in Tim's bed, in the exact same position. I could not sleep, but I was calm. Tim woke up and went to the bathroom and believed he'd disturbed me. I patted the bed: why didn't he come in? I wanted to feel another person close at hand. He mumbled something and went back to the couch, and I lay there, and in the end I was asleep, too, like any other night.

I was aware that I had murdered a man. I was a murderer. It was just that the word, the idea, didn't mean any more than if I remembered I was a woman, or an Irish-American.

That's why it was easy to be composed during the investigation. I had no real fear of being found out. The easy ones to catch – the ones the TV detective pounces on – are the ones who walk around with guilt. You assume all killers are like that, to some extent. The truth will out. The trouble with that statement is that, by definition, you can never know how many truths did not come out.

Also, everyone else was panicking more than me, because they all had secrets that might now emerge: not secrets as big as mine, not in real terms, but just as big to the people hiding them. Jo was scrambling to conceal her drug habit; it might be mild by Dubai standards, but it was still enough to get her locked up if they decided to victimize her. Christian was juggling their financial secrets, more and more precariously. The Fixer, without a passport, wasn't meant to be working there at all. Streng couldn't read. Each one of these elements muddied things. On top of this, as the bloggers all pointed out, the authorities didn't want to see it as a murder. A suicide, or an accidental death-by-excess, was much more convenient for the Dubai story, the story of a utopia where only your own folly could stop you having the time of your life. That was what it became. I knew there'd be another autopsy back in Britain. But I would be long gone by then.

Events worked in my favour. At the golf club, the camera fell so close that it looked like an attempt to silence me. I think Miles pushed it because he knew the WorldWise insurance would pay for a much better replacement camera, and it might be the only way he could get paid. All of us knew by that time that there was no money; except maybe Tim, who hadn't been in the office, who was new to this shambles.

Tim was my alibi, and will be again in the unlikely event that the case ever resurfaces. Knowing already that he was a sleepwalker, I persuaded him that he'd gotten up several times on the night of the murder, and talked to me at around the time Raf was killed. In fact Tim only wandered in once, to use the bathroom, and he barely woke up: he perched on my bed and we exchanged a few words, that was it. I had killed Raf an hour before. The times didn't match at all. But he was drunk enough that he didn't have a clear story in his head, so the story became what I wanted it to be: that some unknown villain had committed the murder, while we, oblivious, slept. It was a bonus that he came to think, in a couple of over-wrought intervals, that he might even have been that villain himself. I don't imagine he still thinks that, even though a complete solution has never come out.

Not even I have a complete solution. I will probably never know who was kissing outside the chalet, though I guess it was Jo and Raf. I'm not certain Miles did push that camera. I don't know why Bradley acted right from the start as if he had something terrible to hide in his room, other than a natural evasiveness. Even the death: I can only tell you why I think I did it. Because my boy got taken, and so many other things happen, and we all go on as if they don't matter, and Raf was especially proud of not caring about anyone, and we were in a place so good at fiction that even a death didn't feel like a big fact.

If I had to say that to his mother? If I ever had to defend myself, explain why I brought sadness into someone else's life as a reaction to my own? I wouldn't be able to justify it. I haven't written this to justify anything.

Last week, after some years with no contact at all, as expected – as planned by me in fact – I happened to get an email from Tim. He and his brother help to run an NGO now, he told me; he's just been to Dubai for a conference. His first time back there. He just felt he ought to get in touch, some-how. Hoped I was all right. He gave me a lot of detail about the company, the conference, his fiancée, about everything. It made me think about all this for the first time; it made me want to write it all down.

Maybe in time I'll reply to Tim, without giving details of where I am. I am all right, I'll tell him. I still produce com-mercials, almost all of them for charities. I live quietly; see few people. Nothing much to report. Of course, there is a little more to the story than that. But it stays with me. I live alongside it, with the knowledge that it's mine.

13: NOW

They left Heathrow on a murky afternoon. Now it is morning again and the city, far below, dazzles as it did seven years ago. When Tim last saw the Burj Dubai – renamed the Burj Khalifa – it was a spindly half-skeleton next to their filming location, hemmed in by humans and diggers and scaffolding. Now it is, as it set out to be, the world's highest building.

Before he came up here Tim stood for a while at the base, trying unsuccessfully to process its extraordinary height, and then made his way around an exhibition which described its design and construction. They built a hexagonal core and then a trio of buttresses in a sort of Y shape, he learned. This allows the building to support itself laterally: to be taller than it was ever thought a building could be. The copy, as usual, suggests it's something more than a building. It is a 'city in the sky'. It's 'iconic', 'legendary', 'Dubai's famous triumph'.

Tim has snapped the view comprehensively, but not very effectively, he feels: his iPhone camera doesn't cope well with the thick layers of architectural glass which separate tourists from the half-mile of empty space between here and the ground. Also, the view is somehow less moving than it ought to be. To be so far above skyscrapers – to see that they're not really scraping the sky, but slouching sullenly in the heat – denudes them of their power. All the billions of dirhams' worth of steel and glass and chrome could be, from here, a model village like Mr Callaghan's in Devon – which, after a financial scare, is in rude health thanks to a recent Lottery grant.

He tries to think how he'll describe the experience to his fiancée Gaby, and to Rod. Although Tim left Facebook a couple of years ago, he still has the reflex – almost ubiquitous in his generation – of experiencing life as a series of status updates, imagining how events will be reported and showcased even while they're still in progress. I'll say it was really impressive, he thinks, even magnificent, but rather impersonal. Perhaps that's what 'iconic' means.

Still, if not emotionally gripping, the view does the job. He can see it all, the city he first gazed on from a much lower vantage point in 2008. There's the glittering coastline, the Burj Al Arab still its inscrutable self. Along from that, he can just about discern the white huts that make up the Village, the Centrepiece – like a child's building block – standing out among them. It did occur to him to stay at the Village, whose website now describes it as 'one of Dubai's most loved institutions' and displays a revised version of the Service Pledge with 'we will bid a fond farewell' tweaked to 'we will say *au revoir* and look forward to the next time!'

In Googling the place, he found very few references to Raf Kavanagh. A documentary was pitched to the BBC by an independent filmmaker, but couldn't get funding as there were so many disputed facts. Raf's family is still active in trying to get a new inquest opened. A benefit fund was set up years ago to 'seek justice' and now has about £30,000 to its name.

In the end, Tim decided against staying there. He went for a second-rate American chain hotel near the Creek. In his time off he has strolled around this area, where the city was born. There are satisfyingly dowdy restaurants, grocers with lurid jars of spices piled high. Old men potter about in dhows, ferrying tourists between points of interest. There is a Metro now, driverless, urged back and forth across the city by unseen hands. That was how he reached the Burj Khalifa this morning. There was an ad in the carriage for Dubai Pearl; a brief investigation satisfied Tim that it was still 'the future of residential Dubai', still 'at the cutting-edge of the world's fastest-growing city', still – like The World – nowhere near finished, let alone sold, or populated.

Google has kept Tim at least loosely abreast of the old

team, even though the whole story is in the past. He knows Bradley and Miles are still working in the business; Miles sends a group email each Christmas, an image of Santa Claus adjusted to show him doing something untoward. Everyone can do this sort of thing these days: image-doctoring skills, which were highly prized when Tim was at Vortex, are almost second nature to the people graduating now. Nobody is surprised if a picture turns out not to reflect reality.

The Ropers live in Hong Kong now: maybe together, maybe separately, or perhaps in a combination of those states, as they did when Tim worked with them. He wrote to them for advice when he and Rod were setting up the NGO, and Christian wrote back with a greatest hits of his favourite rhetorical pieces: there was so much to be done, it was everyone's duty to care. It was not really advice, but in a way it was more valuable; you can never have too many reminders, as Tim likes to tell junior staff, of what is at stake. Besides, it wasn't as if they needed business advice. Rod spends two days a week in the office, and can execute the financial operations with ease. The brothers appeared together only last month in a *Guardian* feature headed 'Keeping It in the Family'; although not Mrs Callaghan's usual newspaper, she bought three copies, and has the article framed next to Tim's wedding invitation, ready to be mounted next time Mr Callaghan has a Sunday away from the model village.

It's only Ruth that Tim has lost track of – Ruth and the Fixer, whom one could never have expected to keep track of, Tim thinks, even when in the same room. It occurs to him that he should try Ruth's old email address; the sight of the Centrepiece, however distant, has stirred something, some almost-buried instinct. The lift bustles down the oesophagus of the building, an ear-popping 163 floors in a couple of minutes. The cityscape rushes towards them, becoming bigger and more solid, and he remembers with faint amusement the atmosphere on that last night, seven years ago: the rumbles of financial disaster, the atmosphere of transience as if the place might evaporate, which made it even easier to succumb to the drunken temptation of a tryst that was over almost as soon as it began.

There was a period, certainly, when it appeared that this *could* all vanish. Chastened money-makers fled the Emirates, dumping cars on waste ground next to the airport, selling real estate at a tenth of its supposed value. Journalists wrote pieces implying that Dubai was a sort of new Roman Empire, impaled on its own ambition. The city was a go-to for the many commentators trying to prove that greed had paralysed civilization. The Ropers were not the only luminaries to sell their Palm mansions.

But a few years on, in 2015, and you would never know there had been a meltdown. The malls and resorts still attract humans doing what humans do: spending money on things they want. 'Financial crisis' is a phrase you hear, like 'civil war': an idea, not a reality. The world, after all, is a very robust construct.

Tim is speaking at a hotel adjacent to the Old Town where they spent a single day filming seven years ago. The mocked-up souk is well established now, though only a smattering of consumers are browsing the stuffed animals in Camel Central or the trinkets in Modern Antiques. There's a collection of restaurants looking out over a large water feature at the foot of the Burj, and he sits at a table, watching the construction vehicles as they jostle lazily. He orders a Coke Life – the newest addition to the Coca-Cola family, containing fewer calories and less sugar than its predecessors, but with a decidedly less nihilistic name than Zero, which they were promoting last time Tim was here. A friend from advertising, working on the account, told him it was more or less the exact same drink re-packaged. A few years ago Tim might have sidestepped it, out of some sense that he was above the tricks of marketing; now those tricks simply don't interest him either way.

He gets out his notes and consults them, like poor old Bradley before the campaign launch that night. It's his first speech at a conference, but he's used to doing presentations; it's a lot easier when you care what you're talking about. The key to tackling inequality, he'll tell the hundred or so people, is convincing the public that small-scale acts are worthwhile. The perception that charities are a 'bottomless pit' comes from the lack of effective communication. (Tim's got a good joke about the 'bottomless drinks' offered in some chain restaurants, which he might slip in here if things are starting to feel a little dry.)

If people hear that a charity has spent a billion pounds, he will say, and then they learn that the relevant area is still rife with poverty or disease, of course they lose faith in the notion that their £10 will help anybody. Good charities make people see the importance of the £10; they make it clear that that money connects individual with individual, across thousands of miles, and that each one of us with a comfortable life has the opportunity – or even the duty – to do good. The duty to care about everybody else. That's the one line Tim has kept from what used to be Christian's spiel.

Our NGO, he'll conclude, provides a free service to help charities articulate the good they are doing. In the last decade it was thought that image, 'brand', was almost more important than the work itself. It didn't just stand for the work. It practically replaced it. Now we realize that—

'How is your stay in Dubai, sir?' asks a diminutive man sidling up beside Tim's table. For a heart-fluttering second it could be Ashraf, but of course, it isn't.

'It's been good, thank you,' says Tim.

It is essential to 'tell a story', but there has to be something beyond the story. And that 'something' has to be real, real in a way that is not just end-of-year reports, or a fancy website: in short, not just words. It has to be something you can reach out and touch.

Tim was thinking of illustrating this by 'reaching out and touching' some sort of prop, maybe the little foam globe he's brought along with him for illustration, but he decides, as he sets out for the hotel, that that would be too tacky. Too style-over-substance. Substance is the whole point. Besides, Rod would never stop taking the piss when he watched the video back.

At the foot of the Burj is an enormous fountain. It cost 800 million dirhams to build. There was a competition to name it: it was won by someone who suggested Dubai Fountain. Every half an hour or so, day and night, it shoots a long series of water-jets into the air, the water dancing through different colours supplied by a few hundred projectors. There is a soundtrack of opera classics which booms out across the plaza, harmonizing with the dance of the water. Hardly anyone looks at it, except during special events; most of the time, it just continues. Tim stops now and watches the fountain spewing out its water. He feels the swell of the music, written by a nineteenth-century composer in honour of a dead friend, on the back of his neck. For a moment he thinks that the centuries-old melody is connecting him with some sort of reality beyond his immediate circumstances; he thinks of Raf's death, two miles from here, with a quick flicker of something like grief, or pity. Then the moment is gone, into the big blue sky, and everything carries on.

picador.com

blog
videos
interviews
extracts